Jake

The Second Novel
of
The Gunpowder Trilogy

Arch Montgomery

**bancroft
press**

Baltimore, MD

Published by Bancroft Press ("Books that enlighten")
P.O. Box 65360, Baltimore, MD 21209
800-637-7377
410-764-1967 (fax)
www.bancroftpress.com

Cover and interior design by Tammy Grimes, www.tsgcrescent.com,
814.941.7447
Cover illustration by Phyllis Montgomery
Author photo courtesy of Patrick Smithwick

ISBN 1-890862-31-2
Library of Congress Control Number: 2004100003
Printed in the United States of America

First Edition

1 3 5 7 9 10 8 6 4 2

*Dedicated with love and admiration
to my mother and father, Anita and Tad Montgomery—
the quintessential school people*

I.

Chapter 1

I'm required to keep a journal. Mom decided I should go to this private school in Baltimore, and they make us do this journal thing. The new school couldn't be worse than my ninth grade year at my totally lame high school here in the county. Boring doesn't begin to describe it. But this journal stuff is bogus. We have to show up in September with a minimum of five thousand words written in our own handwriting. They won't read what we write unless we want them to. They just check to see if we've done it. If we absolutely cannot think of something to say, we can just copy stuff from either Shakespeare tragedies, Frost poetry, the King James Version of the Old Testament, or a David McCullough history book. Jesus, what a waste of a perfectly good summer. They suggest we write about ourselves a little and then just talk about our summer or some stuff we care about. We can even write poetry or short stories.

So here goes.

I'm Jake. I'm fifteen. I'm about five foot eight and three quarters, and it really pisses me off that it looks like I'm about done growing. My mother, Karen, is only about five-four, and I'm told my dad was about five-nine. The only grandparent I've known, Pops, was only about five-seven before he died earlier this summer. You'd think he'd have been taller being a Texan, but he was a shrimp. I come from a family of squirts, so I guess I shouldn't be surprised, but it still pisses me off.

Let me see . . . brown hair, brown eyes, about one hundred and forty-five pounds. I play soccer but I love baseball—second base, only guy to make the varsity as a ninth grader last spring, hit .320. Good student, straight A's, but you'd need to be totally brain-dead to get bad grades at my old school. I think that's why Mom's making me go to this private school, St. Stephen's. I did no work and I didn't have to read much of anything, and it made her completely crazy so she made me take this entrance test. I guess I must have done OK, because this St. Stephen's is supposed to be real selective (I think that means stuck-up), and they took me with a huge scholarship grant because there's no other way we could swing the tuition. It's not my choice, but fighting with Mom, once she's made up her mind on something, is a waste of energy. It's an all boys school for Christ's sake. I'm gonna go crazy without any chicks around. And they bring in kids from all over the city so nobody knows anybody else until they get there. I'm told it's real religious and the work is harder than hell. You've got to wear a blue blazer, a school tie, a button-down blue dress shirt, khaki pants with a belt, brown tie shoes, and dark socks. It sounds like a frigging military academy. I'm guessing that the whole thing'll be a bummer. Maybe it'll be worse than being bored to death up here in the county. Time will tell.

The other thing this school does to totally screw up my summer is reading. We have to get either the Sunday *New York Times* or the Sunday *Washington Post*. Not only do we have to read it, we have to collect all the articles about Europe in a scrapbook. This is some part of their "core curriculum" that they call "Humanities," and in the tenth grade it focuses on Modern Europe and European literature. To make things worse, since I missed their core ninth grade Humanities course, I have to read a ton of books that the class read last year to keep from being behind. I guess they don't take too many kids into tenth grade because they want you to have their whole program. I've gotta read some books called *Poets, Prophets, Priests and Kings*, about the Hebrews, *These Were the Greeks, These Were the Romans*, excerpts from *The Iliad*, and a play called *Antigone*. I'd bag the whole thing but Mom has me on a schedule. I read for two hours every morning. But that's not all. There's the regular summer reading for the tenth grade. I gotta read a book that's all in French. It's *L'Etranger* by a guy named Camus, and it is plenty weird as far as I can understand it. Then I have to read *All's Quiet On the Western Front*—some novel, *The World Lit Only by Fire*—a history book, and *Hamlet*—one of Shakespeare's numbers.

How's that for a great summer?! That sucks is what it does. I've been reading almost around the clock, it seems to me. I'll admit that some of the books are OK, but I hate reading during my summer. How I spend my summer should be none of the school's damn business!

It was almost a relief when Pops died. I know that sounds awful, and I loved him and all that, but he'd been really sick and miserable for about ten months, ever since he had a stroke. Mom and me and my little sister, Steph, went down to Austin for a week when he died. Mom got off my back and I did absolutely zero reading. Excellent! I guess I got all my sadness out when Pops had his stroke. Mom spent lots of time flying back and forth to Austin all year and she said he couldn't speak and couldn't move his right side at all. I have trouble imagining that. He was about as active as an eighty-year-old guy could be. His funeral creeped me out a little. The rest of the week we got to do stuff with Mom that Pops used to do with us whenever we visited him in Austin. It was almost like he was with us.

Jake

We had a picnic just when it was getting dark, near this bridge that goes over Town Lake in Austin. A zillion bats flew out from under it. Pops used to love that. He came down at least once a week, drank a Shiner's Bock beer out of a longneck, which he claimed was a religious experience, and he fished off the bank while watching the bats. It would have been more fun with him there, but it was pretty good just with Mom and Steph.

We went swimming at Barton Springs. Pops did that every week just about year-round and claimed there was no place in the world like it. It's a different kind of place, maybe about a hundred yards long and thirty yards across, but I'm bad on dimensions. Anyway, it's real big. It has grassy banks rising up from dark stone walls. There are lots of good shade trees, and in the summer, the water feels like ice. Pops used to say there was nothing better than Barton Springs to cure the effects of a Texas summer day. Steph and I swam and ran around for about two hours while Mom sat in the shade and watched us. It was great.

Then there was this awesome restaurant where you sit out on a wooden deck and look out over the Texas hill country and eat these unbelievable ribs and brisket and sausage and beans. Pops said it was his favorite place to eat himself sick. That's what Steph and I did. Mom smiled watching us stuff ourselves, and I ate her meal 'cause she didn't have much appetite.

The funeral itself was awful. At least it was short. This little Episcopal Church was packed. Pops had taught in the UT Engineering School for forty years, from shortly after WWII until he was seventy. God, it was hot in there, and in the graveyard, the sun just about baked my brains right through my skull. I admit I didn't hear much of the service—I was pretty much sweating and dehydrating. I did notice that they played "From the Halls of Montezuma to the Shores of Tripoli . . ." which I used to sing with Pops, and I heard the preacher say something about Pops being "a quiet hero not just in war, which we all know about, but also in the dignity with which he lived his life in both good times and bad." I heard the words, "humility, honor, and humanity." I know I should have listened better but it was just so hot.

The only cool thing about the whole thing was the Marine Honor Guard in the cemetery. They handed Mom a folded-up flag with a bunch of medals pinned on it. Then they fired off rifles and a guy played taps. Mom had tears all over her face and kept on leaning over to squeeze my leg and ask me how I was doing. Steph was on the other side of her, and Mom was doing the same thing with her. When the whole thing was over, there was a reception in the Parish Hall, which was air-conditioned. What a relief! Bunches of folks came by to talk to Mom, people who must have known her as a girl in Austin, but there wasn't much for Steph and me to do but drink lemonade and eat these little white bread sandwiches, which I ate a ton of.

We got back home at the end of July. It was damn near as hot in Maryland as it was in Texas. That's the way it's been all August. I've been playing in the Baltimore County Summer Baseball League. That's OK, but our team isn't strong and my play has been marginal. I'm getting way out in front of every off-speed pitch. At least my fielding has held up. I'm actually error free for the season.

Jesus . . . I'm running out of stuff to say and I'm not anywhere close to 5,000 words. Oh, I know another reason this summer sucks. My stepbrother Hank isn't around. He lived at our house about half the time all the way through seventh grade. Then me and him ran into a little trouble, and he spent less time at our house. We saw each other lots during eighth grade again, but then my Mom threw my stepfather, who was Hank's dad, out of the house. It sure took me by surprise. Mom only said that relationships are complicated and this one wasn't working. "We're not going to talk about blame here, Jake. It takes two people to break up a marriage." That was no answer, but Hank called me on the phone and said he was pretty sure that his dad was fooling around with other women. I asked him how he knew, and he said that's how his dad screwed up his first marriage. The explanation makes sense as Mom's about as straight and narrow as you get. Anyway, when they broke up, I saw Hank even less. Then last fall, Hank's mom's new husband got some techie job down in Norfolk, Virginia, so Hank moved away with them. We talked over the phone for a while, but that stopped. Hank was always up for some crazy stuff. He loved his mountain bike and could always think of something goofy to do.

Hank's heart used to get way out in front of his head. It got him and sometimes me in trouble. Like at school, he used to dis the real boring teachers, and he refused to do work that was what he called "too dumb for the dumb." I remember once at an Orioles baseball game, he got all pissed off at some racist redneck yelling stuff at the players. I saw he was getting ready to fight with these big assholes, so I ran and got an usher. Sure enough, Hank started screaming, and the ushers showed up just in time to save his skinny, crazy little butt. How can you do anything but like a kid like that? But he sure didn't think things through. He was like a walking conscience with no brakes. I don't have anybody like that around me these days. I miss him.

The other thing about this divorce is that I can't do what I want 'cause there's no cash. Mom says she got the house, and it's paid off, but that's it. I used to be able to go to movies, and if I wanted stuff, I could pretty much get it. That's over. We eat pasta for every meal, it seems, and Mom spends her life looking for good deals. Being poor sucks. Let's face it, I like money.

So, it's me, Mom, and Steph. What else is there? . . . My real dad. He died before I knew him. Mom was pregnant with Steph when he was killed instantly in a car accident. I was almost three. I keep a picture of him holding me next to my bed. He was a gastroenterologist or something at Johns Hopkins, taught at the medical school, and had a private practice. He and Mom met while they were undergraduates at the University of Pennsylvania. He played baseball at Penn before going to med school at Emory. Mom followed him around while he did residencies and internships and other training type deals, and she found work in publishing houses, or as an editor at magazines, or some such stuff. When I came along she became a full-time mom. She went back to work after she threw my stepfather out. She always seems pissed off and in a hurry. Sometimes it drives me a little nuts.

5,000 words for Christ's sake! What else is there? . . . Oh, it's Labor Day weekend. That's why I'm trying to get this stuff done all at once. I want to have the rest of the weekend free because there's a new kid orientation all day Tuesday, then we do some class thing for the tenth grade on Wednesday, then we have some sort of all-day academic and athletic orientation along with what they call the Opening Convocation on Thursday. On Friday we do a full day of classes. Then on Saturday morning, we're introduced to our community service options, whatever they are, and we do sports in the afternoon. The returning boys will all start sports on Tuesday and have practice Tuesday through Saturday, but us new kids don't go to that. They say sports are real big at St. Stephen's, but they don't believe sports practice should start before school starts up in the fall. They delay their opening games until after the first two weeks of school so the teams can get ready. This all seems pretty weird if you ask me. Out here in the county, the kids have been playing football and soccer for most of August. Sports rule! St. Stephen's is a little behind the times.

What the school does do during August is send out a bunch of letters. Christ, we must have had a dozen of them waiting for us when we got back from Texas, and another bunch have come since then. Most of them were just form stuff, but some of them were a little weird. The principal, which St. Stephen's calls the rector, is this woman named Mary White. Mom read her welcome letter out loud to me, and then we had to talk about it. It was real long and talked about the school's goals and expectations and stuff. They seem to care more about lots of little things that they never talked about out here in the county. And, get this, they've got one rule, no rulebook, no nothing. It's just "Do unto others as you would have others do unto you." That's it. The place must be chaos. We had to sign a form saying that we had read the letter, and that we understood that the school could choose to dismiss a student or not invite a student back "in its sole discretion and for any or no reason." Sounds like if I want to leave, it'll be pretty easy to find my way back to the county.

I admit to being impressed by the little note at the bottom of the letter in the principal's own handwriting. She knew to call me "Jake" and not Jackson, which is my real name, and she hoped I was having fun playing baseball. She apologized that I had extra reading to do because that was a tough load, but it was important to help me have the same background as my classmates so I wouldn't be at a disadvantage. She said good luck, and said she looked forward to seeing me soon. That's pretty cool. I barely ever saw my old principal, though Hank sure saw him a lot more than he wanted.

I also got a letter from my advisor, George Meader, who will teach me Geometry and who is the varsity baseball coach. He sounds pretty cool, has a wife and two kids, has been at the school for thirteen years, and loves to mountain bike. He even called me on the phone, and we talked for about a half-hour. He runs the Environmental Club for Community Services on Saturdays, so maybe I'll sign up for that.

Joel Kohn called me too. He's my student advisor. He sounded pretty cool too, though he says he hates sports and is way into singing and "technical theatre," whatever that is. He says he likes to go up to New York for plays and stuff, and that there's real good music and theatre in Baltimore, too. He called himself "the kike with a mike," and I didn't know what to say. He said, "I'm kidding, man; there's lots of us Jews at St. Stephen's, but we're a minority there like everywhere else, so you gotta laugh." I said, "Whatever." He says he'll take me to this blues club if I want. That'll be good.

Well, I'm guessing I'm within a thousand words of 5,000, and that should be good enough. I've been up most of the frigging night trying to get this done. My scrapbook's done. The books are read. Mom would have driven me completely crazy if I hadn't done that stuff, so there really wasn't much choice.

I'm a little scared about this whole thing. I don't know a single person at this school, and I'm getting the idea that they push students pretty hard. I'm not sure what Mom has gotten me into—all boys, uniforms, stuff you have to do on Saturdays, lots of religious stuff . . . As Dorothy said in Mom's favorite movie, the one that I saw as a kid about a zillion times: "We're not in Kansas anymore, Toto!"

Chapter 2

JULY 20, 2001—COVER SHEET ENCLOSED
WITH ST. STEPHEN'S LETTER

Please read and discuss this letter and its enclosures with your son. Please sign and return the enclosed "statement of understanding."

LETTER TO ALL NEW PARENTS
AND STUDENTS FROM THE RECTOR

Dear Ms. Collins and Jake:

Welcome to St. Stephen's Episcopal School. We are delighted you are joining our extended school community and look forward eagerly to knowing you better. Please do not hesitate to call me, your faculty advisor, or your student advisor before school begins if you have any questions or concerns. We expect you will have plenty of questions, and we understand entirely if you are a bit apprehensive about getting started at a new school.

You should know first and foremost that we are an intimate place. We not only call one another by name, but we also know about and care for one another. Since we ask our students to extend themselves in virtually every area of personal development, we are obligated to support students in a wide variety of ways. Your faculty advisor will see you every day, and you should feel free to rely on him or her, but that's not the only relationship you will be able to count on. All your teachers are expected to be available to you. Call them; ask them for help. Seek advice, or just stop by their offices to talk. All of them will be warm, accessible, and approachable. The same is true of our seniors. We are very proud of them. Before school starts, they go through several days of leadership training at a retreat held on the Eastern Shore of Maryland. They are good sources of information and are ready to help new students. In fact, they will be disappointed if you don't let them be helpful to you.

On a more formal basis, and if you ever feel the need for confidential advice or counseling, you will be able to see one of our two chaplains, our guidance counselor, or our school psychologist, who visits our campus on Monday, Wednesday, and Friday mornings.

We believe this sort of supportive, caring environment is the most conducive setting for boys who are undertaking to develop into thoughtful, caring members of a community. Growth is hard work, and our school may be a little quirky by current cultural standards in believing that any kind of achievement worthy of the name requires such virtues as hard work, courage, persistence, and integrity. Growing up is not risk-free. Failure and hard knocks are part of the process. We all fail at times, but our defining moments come in our reaction to those failures. If you do not suffer some setbacks, disappointments, and even failures at St. Stephen's Episcopal School, we will not have served you well. Likewise, if we are not there to help you dust yourself off and get back on your feet to try again, we are not fulfilling our mission.

In order to create such an environment, we have evolved into a place which might be considered peculiar to some, and we would like to draw your attention to those peculiarities so you will not be surprised by them and so you might even join us in considering them helpful in the pursuit of our mission.

DAILY COMMUNITY WORSHIP AND MEALS

We gather as a community in our chapel every morning at 8:00 a.m., and we break bread together as a community—teachers and students—every day at noon in the Refectory. We consider these all-school gatherings central to our mission. These are times we take to learn about ourselves, one another, and God. These are times for conversation, reflection, and prayer. Since we have in our community not only Protestant and Roman Catholic teachers and students but also members of the Jewish, Moslem, Sikh, Buddhist, and Hindu faiths, we are mindful that our Episcopal tradition gives us "a" view of God, not "the" view of God. This does not require us to abandon our tradition, but it does mandate that we take seriously a wide variety of other traditions. At least once a week, a rabbi, mullah, or person of faith of another tradition leads us in prayer during our morning service. No boy is ever required to participate in anything that violates his conscience, but every boy is expected to be respectful of and open-minded to the traditions and faiths of others. This is a critical aspect of our school, one which we insist upon, and attendance is mandatory.

ACADEMIC PROGRAM

We know there are many good schools which choose to accomplish their various missions in widely divergent ways. It is in humility that we have chosen our path, which we believe is consistent with our goals. It is critical to our success that you understand what we do and why we do it because our approaches are certainly not mainstream. We want you to know precisely what you are getting into. We offer almost no electives. Instead, every boy takes a core curriculum. We believe that adult experts will do a better job of choosing wisely what course of study is appropriate for teenage boys than will teenage boys themselves. We also believe that the nation's institutions of higher education have abandoned even a thin pretense of providing students with a broad, rigorous grounding in liberal arts designed to shape students into humane citizens devoted to truth, goodness, and service.

This leaves secondary schools the job of acquainting our students with those disciplines salutary to development of thoughtful, decent, committed human beings. Consequently, all our students must have a broad and thorough grounding in mathematics through calculus, all three core science disciplines (physics, chemistry, biology); exposure to Western and Non-Western history, literature, religion, art, and music; a foreign language to competence; community service; and athletics. Boys must write often. They must give oral reports. They must do independent research, and they must be prepared to defend their scholarship before a panel of teachers at least once a year.

As a corollary to our belief in this broad core curriculum, we want you to understand that we are not a college preparatory school. That phrase appears nowhere in our materials and is not contained in our school mission. We believe that a school only diminishes itself when it is reduced to a mere stepping stone to higher education. We impoverish ourselves when we dilute our mission to a breeding ground for some "name" institution. We are unpersuaded by arguments that we must adjust our curriculum and broad program to meet the demands of selective colleges. Our boys go on to higher education at a level entirely appropriate to their abilities, achievements, and interests.

Sixty-one out of seventy-three seniors last spring were admitted to the institution of their first choice. More importantly, our records indicate that our boys' success during college and afterwards more than justifies our faith in our approach. It is critical that you understand our approach to avoid a misunderstanding in the future.

Finally, we have no grade inflation. If your son is an accurate, original, inventive, persuasive, brilliant, and highly articulate scholar, he may achieve high honors, which is an "A." If his work is close to perfect but not original, he will achieve honors, which is a "B." If, like most boys, your son does good work, meaning that he demonstrates mastery and understanding of the material covered in the course, he will receive a "C." A "D" indicates that your son has passed the course with an acceptable level of accomplishment. An "F" is a failure. We are explicit on the subject of grades because almost all our boys come to us with few if any grades below an "A." We believe that achievement is only worthwhile if it is real, and we reject the notion of "feel good" education where every child receives a gold star, warranted or not.

ATHLETICS

We believe in the value of athletics because they reveal character and help boys to learn about discipline, hard work, courage, perseverance, resilience, cooperation, selflessness, competitive spirit, self-restraint, sportsmanship, and grace under pressure. We believe athletics, done properly, develop life-long habits of health and fitness. Having said that, we believe that competitive athletics at the professional level have developed into puerile entertainment similar to professional wrestling, and Division I college athletics are not far behind. We have athletics at our school for their educational purpose and for no other reason. Consequently, you will notice no team can practice more than ninety minutes a day and never after 6:00 p.m. Practices are never allowed on Sundays. Interscholastic games may be played only on Wednesday afternoon, Friday night, or Saturdays. We will travel no more than one hour to play a game, and absolutely no practices are permitted during school vacations. Athletics will never intrude upon the academic day.

Our athletes are students first, and are offered no more recognition or status than students engaged in any other activity. Although others are surprised, we are not startled to note that most of our teams maintain winning records and earn a healthy share of championships, and that our students often leave us to enjoy success at the highest level of collegiate and international sport. We will not pander to what we believe is society's wrong-headed overemphasis on athletics and winning.

We emphasize this very strongly because sports seem in this day and age to make people crazy. Please notice that this is not a subject on which we are likely to compromise, and if you disagree with us, we are not the right school for you. Note also that we insist not only upon good sportsmanship from both fans and players, but also upon graciousness and generosity of spirit.

THE "RULE," CONDUCT, AND DISCIPLINE

There is big stuff and little stuff, and we don't want to "sweat the small stuff." Consequently, on petty things like appearance, attendance, and promptness, we spend very little time. We have opted for complete clarity and simplicity. We recognize that our requirements in this area are somewhat arbitrary, as are virtually all societal and cultural norms. Nonetheless, rules help promote order, and an orderly school serves our purposes here. You have received our appearance code and dress code by mail. It is clear. It is your responsibility to adhere to it. I shake the hand of each student as he enters chapel every morning. If he is not dressed properly, he goes home. He will be welcome at school the next day if dressed properly. Boys can choose not to attend class. They will suffer the consequences of their poor choice. Boys will not be allowed to enter a class late.

To "big stuff"—discourtesy, unkindness, disruption, physical altercations, dishonesty in any form, law-breaking—we apply our only written rule, which is the Golden Rule. We meet with a student and rarely impose punishment. Instead, we spend a significant amount of time discussing the situation with the boy, his faculty advisor, his senior advisor, the chaplain, the counselor, and other interested parties. We determine why the boy is behaving the way he is, and we develop a plan of action for improvement. We then monitor subsequent behavior. We reserve the right to decide, with or without a stated reason, that a boy's separation from St. Stephen's, either for a period of time or permanently, is in the best interest of either the school or the student or both. We believe that persuasion, not punishment, is the most effective form of discipline, but when we conclude that persuasion is unlikely to prevail, separation is the best answer.

We have no locks at our school—not on lockers, not on doors. Boys come and go as they please. We honor a boy's word and expect him to honor ours. Most boys quickly decide they like this place, and they want to stay. We have very few disciplinary issues. We hope to receive and will insist upon your enthusiastic support for and cooperation with our "rule" and our process.

You will find several enclosures with this letter. Please read them. Please also sign the "Statement of Understanding," and return it to the school in the enclosed envelope. We eagerly look forward to your arrival at St. Stephen's and hope your remaining weeks of summer are restful, productive, and fun.

Sincerely,
Mary White
Rector, St. Stephen's Episcopal School

Handwritten Note on Bottom of the Letter

Dear Jake,

We do look forward to having you join us. Sorry about the heavy reading load, but it is often hard to catch up to the ninth graders who were with us last year given that they enjoy a common core of knowledge. We know you are bright and able—plenty able—to flourish with us. I hope you are able to play some baseball this summer. Your advisor, Mr. Meader, says you love the game and will help us out in the spring.

Yours truly,
Ms. White

Description

St. Stephen's Episcopal School is an Episcopal Church School, founded in 1877, for no more than three hundred boys in grades nine through twelve, located on a twenty-five acre campus within Baltimore City. A twenty-member Board of Trustees is responsible, through the school rector, for perpetuating the mission of the school and for school governance. The faculty, under the guidance of the rector, is responsible for carrying out the school mission.

MISSION

St. Stephen's Episcopal School strives in humility to educate students so that they desire and are able in both heart and mind to undertake a courageous, life-long pilgrimage to discover meaning in their lives through the persistent and earnest effort to know truth, do good, love their fellow man, and serve God.

To that end, the school seeks bright, energetic boys who will be susceptible to the influence of a dedicated, experienced faculty and who will benefit from a rigorous and broad liberal arts curriculum that demands of students that they think hard, feel deeply, and engage fully in an integrated program of academics, service, reflection, and athletics.

THE SCHOOL RULE

Do unto others as you would have them do unto you.

MOTTO

Virtute et numinem: Courage and the light of God, or Grit and Grace

STATEMENT OF UNDERSTANDING

We have read together (parent(s)/guardian(s) and son) the rector's letter of welcome along with the St. Stephen's Episcopal School "Description," "Mission," and "The School Rule." We understand all that we have read and we agree to support the school mission and to strive to follow the school rule.

We further understand and support the principle that the school should be and is the sole interpreter of the school rule, and we agree with and support the school's exercise of unrestricted sole discretion in enforcing the rule. The school will discipline students within that unrestricted sole discretion, and students will be allowed to withdraw from school, dismissed from school, or not invited to return to school for any or no reason. We agree to and understand all of the above as a condition of matriculation at St. Stephen's Episcopal School.

_____

Signature: Parent/Guardian

_____

Signature: Parent/Guardian

_____

Signature: Student

Chapter 3

JOURNAL ENTRY: SEPTEMBER 9, 2001

Mr. Meader doesn't miss much. My summer journal entry looked short to him, so this entry has to be longer. Jeesh, they never would have even checked or noticed out in the county. Writing lots this time shouldn't be too rough because it's been one full and weirded-out week since school started. I got plenty to say. We are required to write a minimum of a thousand words in our journals every week. Bummer. Our advisor will check on Monday mornings, and I get the feeling that they do what they say around here.

Anyway, I show up on Tuesday at 7:45 a.m. all duded out in this military style outfit. I walk up the front steps, making sure there's no marks on my face where Mom must have kissed me about a million times . . . What's with her, crying and stuff like I'm leaving for the moon? I pull open the door of the school. There's this little gray-haired lady standing there smiling at me. I start to walk by her but she holds out her hand so I have to stop, and she says, "Hello, my name is Mary White. I'm the rector here at St. Stephen's. Welcome!"

I mumble something back and start past, but she doesn't let go of my hand. "My guess from seeing your picture in the file is that you are Jake Phillips."

"Yes," I say, and she's looking at me with these bright blue smiling eyes.

She says, "Well, you've just encountered our morning routine. Every day, you'll have to grab my hand, look me in the eye, and address me by name. I'll greet you the same way, and by the way, you look great. We're pleased to have you with us. Now . . . your senior advisor is up there on the landing. He'll start you on your way. Just tell Peter, the boy at the desk over there, your name, and he'll get you fixed right up. Good luck, and stop by my office any time."

This guy Peter sees me when I approach his desk, and he stands up and holds out his hand. "Hi, I'm Peter. Can I help you find your advisor?"

I say "yeah" and give him my name, and he calls out, "Joel!" after looking at a sheet of paper. Over comes this tall skinny kid with a gigantic Adam's apple and a head of hair that's all curls and out of control like some kind of over-fertilized bush. He wears thick glasses, and he walks up on his toes like he's suddenly going to take off skipping or just bounce right out of the room. He holds out his hand, too. This may be the most hand-shaking place I've ever seen in my life. Joel takes me on a tour of the school and, boy, he's gonna make it someday as some kind of comedy man. He's got an opinion on just about everything and everyone, and he barely takes a breath for fifteen minutes. Then he stops in the middle of the hall and says, "Got any questions?"

"Nope," I say 'cause there's just been way too much information for me to even start to remember.

He says, "OK, then, this is your faculty advisor's office, Mr. Meader. He's my advisor, too."

He knocks on the door, and this real low voice says, "Come in."

Joel opens the door, sticks his head in the office, and says, "Your favorite advisee is here along with some new meat for the grinder."

Jake

"Mr. Kohn," the low voice says as Joel opens the door, "go play in traffic and leave us alone before you give me a migraine."

I see a short, wide guy with a gray beard and glasses getting up from a desk piled about two feet high with papers. He's smiling in our direction and comes over and . . . you guessed it—shakes my hand. "You've gotta be Jake," he says.

He shows me to a chair next to his desk as Joel says, "Catch you later," and leaves. The office looks like a warehouse for books, papers, and baseball stuff. There's no way to sit on the couch under the window because there must be several dozen folders, a catcher's mask, a bunch of bats, and some sort of computer stuff all jumbled up. There're pictures of teams on the walls and a picture of Cal Ripken with Mr. Meader. There're trophies on the shelves along with a bunch of signed baseballs and more books and papers and other junk. I step over stacks of books and papers to get to the chair, and I sit down.

The talk's OK. He goes over all my classes—European Humanities, which I guess is a combination of English, History, Art, Religion, and Music; Geometry, which Mr. Meader is going to teach; Physics, which most guys in my class took last year but I have to take in tenth grade to satisfy the Physics, Chemistry, Biology sequence they've set up; French II; and Studio Art, which is a minor course meeting only twice a week. They've got this rotating schedule that makes no sense at all. I've got a ninety-minute Humanities block that meets at different times every day. Then I've got fifty-five minute class periods for all my other classes, with one ninety-minute period once a week attached to my Physics class that they call a lab. The whole thing is completely confusing, and I'll just have to carry this little scheduling card around with me until I get it straight.

We talked about what I liked to do. Other than baseball and messing around in the Gunpowder, fishing and stuff, or riding my bike, I didn't have much to say. Mr. Meader said that if I liked the Gunpowder River, maybe my community service obligation could be satisfied in the Environmental Club, which cleans up the Jones Falls and monitors water quality and stuff. If I have to screw up my Saturdays, doing it in a river might beat some old age home or a soup kitchen. I'm going to hate losing my Saturdays for some sort of do-gooder project, but my options are limited here.

Then Mr. Meader talked to me about grades and rules and the honor code and stuff like that. I knew most of it already because Mom wouldn't leave me alone until we'd read the materials enough times to make me want to toss my cookies. But Mr. Meader did talk a lot about the whole honor thing, talking a lot about what plagiarism is, and how to use Internet resources. He also talked about the difference between group work, which the school likes and encourages, and personal work, which has to be done alone, with specific credit given to any source other than my own ideas. I admit to thinking his real sincere speech about honesty, honor, and integrity was a little funny. Like, what world is this guy living in? He sounds exactly like Mom, and she's a definite extraterrestrial. All these nice little values that they talk about might be good stuff on their planets, but here on earth folks abandoned the good ship "Honest Abe" a long time ago. When I was a lot younger, all that "Slick Willy" Clinton stuff happened, and he's still everybody's hero. When I was even smaller, nobody talked about anything but O.J. Even people who say they care about all these values kick them over when they're in a tight spot. It's every man for himself when it comes to saving your own ass, and as far as I can tell, it's always been that way. Anyway, Mr. Meader seems to believe all this stuff, or if he doesn't, he ought to get an Oscar. So I look back at him real sincere while he's talking, but inside I'm kind of smiling to myself.

When we're finally done, Mr. Meader takes me down to the

Jake

chapel, and all the new ninth graders and the few of us new tenth graders are put in the first three or four rows. That's when Mary White walks in. She has this gentle voice that sounds soft but you can hear it real clear even in the fourth row where I'm sitting. Her eyes are real light blue and she seemed to be looking straight at me the whole time she talked. I didn't dare look away. She told us who she was and that she'd been rector of St. Stephen's for twenty-three years. It strikes me as a little strange that this little old chick is running an all boys' school, but she's managed to stick around the place forever, so she must know what she's doing. Her talk went over the same stuff Mom had said, the same stuff that Mr. Meader had said, and the same stuff that was in all the letters and pamphlets the school sent over the summer. Enough already! But I have to admit there's something about Ms. White that makes you listen even if you don't want to. Maybe it's those eyes. They're like magnets. Whatever it is, you have to pay attention.

When we're done with the speech, we go into the Refectory. It's a big dark wood room with a high ceiling that has beams across it. The windows are arched and have real little panes of glass that are kind of warped or something, so the stuff outside looks curvy, like in one of those fairground mirrors. There are panels on the wall, and every class has a panel with each boy's name carved into it. There are huge pictures of all the past rectors, all mean-looking old guys with white preacher collars and black robes and colorful stuff on their shoulders. I don't know how you can hold down your food with all those dead guys staring at you. All the tables are round, and I sat at one with Mr. Meader and Joel. The food wasn't half bad—burgers and fries—and I scarfed down two burgers. Joel got onto the topic of the Jones Falls Clean-Up Project and must have talked without breathing and with a full mouth for about half an hour. He's the senior leader and seems to think it's a great way to spend a Saturday. "Beats the hell out of

Synagogue," he said, "but my father still makes me go to Friday night services. It sucks!" This guy Joel is one piece of work!

After lunch, Joel takes me down to the Athletic Center. He says he stays as far away from the place as he can get, says he doesn't want to get calluses on his brain, or become a knuckle dragger, or start to crave protein milk shakes. He says the athletic requirement applies to him, though, and tennis seems to be the least objectionable form of sport. He seems to think the fitness program sucks. "Can you imagine," he says, "spending one more minute than you absolutely have to running laps in a circle or pushing some ludicrous piece of metal up and down over and over again? Why would anybody do that on purpose when they could be making music or just screwing around somewhere?" But Joel introduces me to the equipment guy, helps me get the stuff I need for soccer, and then put it in my assigned locker. We go up to the Athletic Director's office and Joel introduces me to this little sawed-off man with short gray hair named Mr. Demeuth. He gives Joel some crap about athletic participation, and Joel laughs and throws it right back at him. We meet a bunch more people, too many to remember, and they all know Joel by name, and he knows them, even though he claims he hates athletics.

That pretty much wraps up the day. Mom picks me up and we drive forty-five minutes out 83 and home. Stephanie is part way up the hill, and we stop to pick her up. She likes the bus to drop her off by the bridge over the Gunpowder so she can mess around playing "Pooh sticks" before walking up the hill to our house. She's full of energy, as usual, and has a lot to say, as usual, so she starts right in talking all the way into the garage, out of the car, and into the kitchen. I don't think she actually said anything. She was cuter when she was littler. Over the last few years, she's become a pain—wants to hang out with me all the time. There's some stuff that a little sister just can't do. She follows me around like a puppy and it just bugs me, that's all. She and Mom seem to have some special code between them where they can communicate without words or signs. That drives me nuts.

Wednesday was tenth grade orientation, and all in all, it wasn't a bad day for me. An Outward Bound Instructor met us at school, and we got in buses and went to Leakin Park where there's an awesome ropes course. They had us divide into teams, where we had to play a bunch of games to make us learn everyone's name and to make us rely on each other to get some job done. It was actually pretty cool. We spent a bunch of time talking about how we did stuff and what did or did not work. I really liked this challenge where we had to get ourselves over a wall that was about fifteen feet high. We completely screwed it up and couldn't get this last fat kid up and over, so we had to start all over. Instead of just starting in the second time, we spent time talking it through. We did it real fast. I met some good kids, and since I'm one of the only new guys, it was nice that they were so friendly. By the end of the day, everybody knew my name and I think I knew most of theirs, too.

Our tenth grade advisor, Mr. Morcomb, did everything with us. There were about five other teachers, too, who are on the tenth grade committee who did this stuff with us. They all seemed to know who I was. Mr. Morcomb is no athlete, I'll tell you that, but he didn't seem to mind making a fool of himself in front of all of us. Neither did the other teachers. He turns out to be chair of the Music Department— plays the piano and the violin and sings with a bunch of groups. I wonder what they had to do to make those teachers come out and do stuff they hate with a bunch of fifteen-year-old kids. Their teachers' union must be pretty weak, or they must pay these teachers a fortune because you wouldn't catch my old teachers in the county doing this kind of stuff.

Thursday was real different and made me wonder what I'd gotten into. After Mom dropped me off, I went to my locker as they'd told me to yesterday and opened it up. There was a little box inside and a loose-leaf notebook. I opened the notebook and the first page said, "Welcome to St. Stephen's, Jake, from the senior class. We're glad you're here. Included on the following sheets are your chapel seat location, your itinerary, and a variety of other pieces of useful information for the day. Just take this notebook with you and refer to it if you are confused. You can ask anybody for help at any time. Good luck, and please open the small box. It has the school lapel pin, which we hope you will want to wear on your blazer as a token of our pleasure that you have joined us and as a reminder of the high standards to which we all aspire. Go forward with *Grit and Grace*! See you in chapel."

I don't remember ever seeing anything like that note, which was supposedly from students. So I put the pin on and headed for chapel. I could hear organ music getting louder as I walked down the hall toward the common room. A line was backed up at the chapel entrance, and when I got to the front, I saw why. Ms. White was shaking the hand of each student and having a little conversation with him. She not only knew them all by name, she also knew what they'd done over the summer and what sport they were playing. When it was my turn, she said, "Hello, Jake Phillips, I understand you did well yesterday on the ropes course. It's hard being new in the tenth grade, but you're off to a good start. I'm betting you'll make a good contribution to our soccer program. Welcome." Then she let go of my hand and I started down the aisle between the old wooden pews that face forward for the first several rows but then face each other across the aisle about half way down. An older boy came up beside me and asked, "Do you know where you're going?"

"Not really," I said.

"New?"

"Yup."

"Thought so. The information is in your notebook. Who's your advisor?"

"Mr. Meader."

"You'll sit with him, then. I'll show you the spot." It was almost all the way down near the altar on the right, in the front row facing across the aisle. I sat down. Everyone was quiet and the organ just seemed to get louder and louder. Then it stopped. The chapel was almost full, but there was silence. I looked toward the back of the chapel and I could see a crucifer, who was wearing a red robe with a white gown over it, standing there with the cross. Guys with lighted candles were on either side of him, and other guys had flagpoles—one had a flag with the school crest on it, another had a Maryland flag, and the third had an American flag. The silence was broken by Ms. White's voice, which filled the chapel clear as a bell, even though I couldn't see where she was standing.

"Let our 173rd academic year begin with the singing of our school hymn, 'O God Our Help in Ages Past.'"

Then the organ crashed in again, and the crucifer started down the aisle. We all stood and started to sing, and I mean everybody sang. The choir followed the crucifer, then the chaplains, and then Ms. White, who walked next to an old guy with a limp. She was dressed in some kind of academic robe. The faculty was all following her in, all dressed in robes, too. They would peel out of the procession to sit with their advisees, so Mr. Meader was about the only teacher left when the procession got all the way to me. He winked at me and squeezed into the space to my left. Around the fourth verse, I looked back toward the rear of the chapel, and here come the seniors. They are wearing striped blazers, which I learn afterwards are the mark of having become a senior. They walk down the aisle two-by-two, singing the hymn, and the president of the student body stops at the front so the whole group of them is stalled out in the aisle stretching from the front to the back of the chapel. We're just finishing up the last verse and going into the Amen with all of them standing there, when Ms. White leaves her place near the altar and stands in front of them. When the organ stops, the place is silent again, except for some kid coughing in the back.

Ms. White says real loud and serious, "You are the class of 2002. You are our leaders and our models. We expect from you integrity, responsibility, kindness, and example. We expect you to demonstrate to our younger students through thought, word, and deed those qualities that make for human beings of high character. We have complete confidence in you. We are proud of you. May God bless this class of 2002. May he protect you and guide you. May he give you strength to choose the hard right over the easy wrong. May he lift you up when you fall. May he keep you humble in triumph. This we ask in the name of Jesus Christ our Lord, who taught us to say . . ."

Then we said the Lord's Prayer. After a brief pause, Ms. White says, "Class of 2002, take your seats, which are emblematic of the leadership of the school."

The seniors then turned and walked up to the top level of the facing pews on both sides, and took their seats in what seemed to be recesses carved into the stone wall of the chapel above and behind the facing pews. We were literally surrounded by the seniors above us.

We sang another hymn. There was a reading by one senior from the Old Testament, and then one from the New Testament. Then another hymn. Ms. White then gets up and introduces the old guy who walked in with her as the chairman of the Board of Trustees. Mr.-

Jake

I-Can't-Remember-His-Name said a few things like how proud he was of the teachers and students and to be a part of such a wonderful school, blah, blah, blah . . . At least his talk was short.

Ms. White gets back up and she talks for longer, but boy she's hard not to listen to. You'd actually have to make a real effort not to pay attention. That's a little spooky. She said lots of stuff about the history of St. Stephen's and its values and its distinctive approach to education. But then she switched to this talk about "love," about how it is the central message of Jesus Christ, that God loves us and that we should love each other as we love ourselves. She said that love was not easy and that it should not be confused with softness intellectually, spiritually, or physically. "To love well and completely is a demanding task that's not for the faint of heart," she said. She said that she loved us, certain times more than others, but always she loved us. The foundation of all the programs at the school—the high standards, the tough work load—all stemmed from the foundation of love for the students by God, by His son, by the trustees, administration, teachers, and staff.

That was pretty heavy stuff, and like Mr. Meader's talk about honor, she seemed to mean it. But you can't laugh inside when Ms. White's doing the talking. I have to admit, though, that the message is a little far out. How can she love us when she can't possibly even know us?

When Ms. White finishes, we sing a hymn and go through the entire Holy Communion bread and wine number. About half the boys in the school don't go up for communion, but I do because I'm Episcopal. When that's all done, Ms. White gets up and says the traditional welcome by the senior class will now begin. With that, the organ goes crazy again, and we start to sing yet another hymn while the seniors walk down from their seats and leave. The faculty follows them, then the choir, and finally the cross, the priests, the flags, Ms. White, and the old guy with the limp. We then follow them out two-by-two, starting from the front, with the organ still real loud.

When I get outside the chapel, I see a line of seniors stretching from the chapel through the common room and around a corner. The first guy, the student body president, reaches out and shakes my hand, says he's Peter Randolph, and asks my name. I tell him and he passes me onto the next senior. And that happens with every senior all the way around the corner, and now I see the faculty is all lined up, and the same thing happens with them until I get all the way past the classrooms to the Refectory. There, Ms. White shakes my hand again and says to please come in for the morning tea before we break for classes. In I go, and there are all kinds of food, from doughnuts and pastries to sandwiches. There's juice and coffee and tea, and everybody's milling around and eating and talking. Pretty weird.

Guys say hello to me and ask me how it's going. Joel comes up after awhile, and he says, "How'd you like the Royal Welcome? Pretty British, whot, whot? Expect to see the old queen parachute in with the Archbishop of Canterbury at any second? Tea anyone? Ta-ta." And he was off in his striped blazer. Mr. Meader had been standing there listening and smiling as Joel gave me his spiel. "A character, that one," he said. "One of the finest young men in school—an independent thinker with a good heart."

"Oh," I said.

Mr. Meader smiled at me and asked, "Are you a little overwhelmed?"

"Yup," I say, and that was true. I'm not sure what to make of this whole thing, and I'm beginning to wonder if I'm in the right place. A loud chime rang, and everyone started to leave at once. It was time for classes. I went to my locker, got my notebook, read the first page, and

Jake

headed off for European Humanities.

We only had a half-hour in each class. The teachers gave us materials and books. They explained expectations, grading systems, and other stuff. They each went over the first assignment, which would be due the next day, Friday. When all that was done, we went to lunch in the Refectory. We stood behind our chairs until the chimes rang, and then everyone got quiet. Peter, the student body president, said grace, and then we all sat down at once. Every student sits with his advisors, so I sat there with Joel and Mr. Meader and seven other kids around one of those big round wooden tables that seats ten of us. A senior waited on the table and brought us a big bowl of spaghetti, a bowl of salad and a huge basket of bread. Mr. Meader ladled the stuff out on plates and we passed them around. No one started to eat until Mr. Meader said, "Fall to it, gentlemen." I watched our senior waiter in his striped blazer standing against the wall. Kind of weird that the seniors are supposed to be the leaders, but they have to wait on tables. I asked Joel about it, and he said that seniors always wait on the tables for the first month of school. Then the juniors take the job for a month, then the sophomores, and then the freshmen. That gets the school all the way to Christmas, and for the rest of the year, the underclassmen and teachers all rotate the job between them.

Dessert was an ice cream sundae, which was excellent. Then there were announcements. After that, we broke for a one-hour study period. Sophomores were allowed to go to the library, to several designated study areas, to a computer lab, or to the common room. School is intended to be quiet during this period. We went from there to athletics, and I had an OK time running around on the soccer field.

Mom picked me up. Man, has she been grouchy lately. She's a little embarrassing, too, because she's looking pretty ratty. You'd think she'd fix herself up a little, but no—she has the look of a person who can't quite get it all together, which is kind of unnatural for her. But tired looking as she is, she can still work up the energy to nag me nuts. She's still her old self there. She wants me to tuck my shirt in, sit up at the table, not chew with my mouth open. Blah-blah. Dinner was one correction after the next. Even Stephie started to squirm. God, what a pain! Hank used to call Mom the perfect lady, and she's getting to be less perfect and ever more of a pain. What's with the big circles under her eyes, too? She looks like a raccoon. She stays up all night working. You'd think she'd give it a break and get a life. Maybe if she'd chill out, go to dinner or to a movie or something, she'd ease up on me a little. She's got me in her sights, boy, and that's not the place to be. She needs to just mellow!

Friday was a full day of classes. In every class, we sat around a huge table. There's a laptop computer at every seat, a screen at one end of each room, and a projector that hooks onto the computers. White boards and bulletin boards are on the walls. My biggest class is Humanities, which has twelve kids in it.

My smallest is French, which has eight of us. The teachers already know us all by name. Everybody talks in every class. It's like a big conversation. Even in Physics and Geometry, there's a group discussion, and everybody tries to solve problems in teams. French was awful, though. You couldn't say anything in English. Nothing. You'd think the teacher might not even know English, except I heard him talking it yesterday.

The weirdest class is this Humanities thing. Two teachers do it together. One is an expert in British Literature, and the other has a doctorate in history with a concentration on Germany. He speaks German, too. The two of them will teach the course most of the time, but the Chaplain will come in every couple of weeks to lecture us on religion. So will the chairs of the Art and Music Departments. On top of that . . . get this . . . we go on a ton of field trips. Here in Baltimore, we'll go to the Walters Art Gallery and the Baltimore Museum of Art about six times. Then we'll hear the Baltimore Symphony Orchestra twice, operas at the Lyric twice, and chamber orchestra stuff at the Peabody twice. We'll have field trips down to Washington twice to a place called the Corcoran and to the Smithsonian, and we'll even hit the Kennedy Center. They'll take us to the Holocaust Museum, too. In a two-day trip to New York City, we'll visit a ton of museums, watch a ballet, and hear some big-name tenor at Carnegie Hall. All this stuff is a required part of the course.

I guess that sounds OK, but the reading load is pretty scary. We use lots of original documents, and lots of what they call secondary sources. We don't get a regular textbook, and I asked about that, but the teachers said not to worry—we'd be given all the facts and figures we needed to learn through hand-outs and lectures. I guess you have to take great notes. Everything gets handed in and then corrected by computer. Then we can redo work till we think it's good enough, and then it goes into this special portfolio of work. The teachers said that would be up to us after several back and forths with the teacher. Once we are satisfied that something is our best work, we could put it into the portfolio. All our assessments would be based on the totality of our portfolio, and we always have the option to go back and redo stuff even after it's been graded in the portfolio.

If that isn't a strange way of doing things, I don't know what is. In the county, you'd get a test, circle the right multiple choice answer or fill in the blank, and then you'd get back your grade about two weeks later. That seems like a more sensible way of doing things. This portfolio stuff sounds like a complicated mess.

After soccer practice Friday, I was tired. It was six when Mom picked me up. I'd been wondering about getting my learner's permit and about Driver's Ed, which I'm old enough to take now, so I asked her. She was acting strange, though, and didn't seem to want to talk. She was sitting kind of hunched over the steering wheel. About two minutes after I ask her the question, we're already on the Jones Falls Expressway, and she looks over at me like she was coming out of some sort of trance, and says, "Sunday's your only free day. Look into it. Find out how much it costs and what I have to do. Then we'll talk. If you're old enough to drive, you're old enough to figure this out yourself."

Thanks a bunch for all the help, Mom, I'm thinking to myself. She shoves me into this school, takes a job that has her acting like a zombie, and then throws everything in my direction. Don't parents usually take care of this kind of stuff for their kids? Well, if that's the way it's going to be . . . fine!

Stephie's running around like a maniac when I get home, and she wants to play around, but I just want to chill out in front of the tube. Mom asks, "What time do you have to be at school on Saturday?"

Stephie says, "School on Saturday? Who has to go to school on Saturday?"

"Jake does."

So she starts to sing over and over again, "Jake has to go to school on Saturday, Saturday, Saturday. Jake has to go on Saturday, all day long," until I'm ready to strangle her. Being me in my house is not great these days.

So, when I do show up on Saturday at 8:00 a.m., I'm in a pissy mood. Mom drove me, and we said nothing all the way in. She looked her usual worn-out self. I went over to Joel, who was holding a sign that said "Jones Falls Clean-Up," and just stood there. He was calling out everybody's name and telling them how much fun they'd have if they came with him. About eight other guys gathered around him, so he finally said, "That's it, then. Let's go."

We walked around behind the gym towards some vans, where some teachers were standing, talking, and drinking coffee. I was walking with Joel a little behind the others and I said half under my breath, "This sucks big time."

Joel stopped walking and put his hand on my shoulder to let the others pass. "Don't do it then, man. Go do something you like better. There's a bunch of choices here."

"Yeah, right," I say real sarcastic. "It's not that. It's being here at all on a Saturday. What kind of shit is that?"

Joel looked at me for awhile and finally said, "You don't get this place at all, do you?"

"What?" I said.

"Why are you here?"

"Because my mother made me come."

"Then you should leave," he said. "There's lots of kids who wanted to be here and couldn't get in. You're just taking up space."

"I can't."

"Why not?"

"My mother would kill me."

"If I go to Meader and tell him you want to leave, and if he tells that to Ms. White, your mother won't have any say. You'll be gone. They don't want kids who don't want to be here."

I didn't say anything.

Joel started in again, "Look, I like this stuff. It means a lot to me, trying to clean up this nasty little fucked-up stretch of water. This is real. I don't want you around if you're going to cop an attitude. So make up your mind."

I didn't say anything, and he let go of my shoulder and started toward the vans. I followed him. This guy's more like a teacher than a kid sometimes. It pisses me off. The whole thing pisses me off.

We went to a part of the Jones Falls near this old mill and we picked up paper for two hours. Now, there's a great way to spend time. Joel was running all over the place like he was the happiest little moron in the world. This is one screwed-up way to spend a Saturday.

Saturday night, I vegged out, and Sunday morning I slept in. I guess Mom figured I got enough religion at school, so I didn't have to go to church with her and Steph. At about eleven, I got up and ate about a loaf of raisin bread, and then I started doing all this homework. By three, I was done.

I grabbed a sandwich and a glass of milk before heading out toward the Gunpowder on my bike. I took my fishing gear. It's actually Dad's. I found it up in the attic last year. Hank and I used to make fun of the fishermen, but I tried out some of the stuff and read this book that was in with the gear called *Fly Fishing for Beginners*. It turns out to be a whole lot easier than those doofesses on the Gunpowder make it look. I've gotten good, and I really like it. Nobody bothers you. It's in a nice place. You can think random stuff, not think at all, or actually think about catching fish. It was about time something good happened this week. I caught a nice twelve- or thirteen-inch brown with a gold ribbed hare's ear bouncing along the bottom. Nice.

Not nice is tomorrow. We start in with chapel just like every day, and we'll see how it goes. The seniors start in on Monday with their chapel convocations. Every senior is required to give one. How lame is that?! Well, I can always daydream through the bad ones.

This is enough writing. I had lots to say. Mr. Meader can't complain. This is way over the requirement, so screw him.

Chapter 4

Welcome back, gentlemen, to our 124th year. I'm glad to see you all, and I trust you've had invigorating summers that have left you eager for the challenge ahead, which is the 2001-2002 academic year at St. Stephen's Episcopal School. Please drop by my office and fill me in on anything exciting or interesting that you've done. For those of you who are new to St. Stephen's, I offer you a special welcome. As you come to know us, I believe you will find us warm, accessible, and helpful. If you have a problem, ask for help. St. Stephen's School asks a lot of its students, but it also gives a lot.

That is what this school has done since its founding in 1877. The school was small at its inception and, as dictated by its formal mission, it has remained small, in the belief that close contact between teacher and student is the key to shaping youngsters in any lasting or significant way. We know it is possible to merely teach academics in larger settings, but we do not want to diminish our mission by restricting it to accomplishing technical competence in academic disciplines. That is important, of course, and we try to do it well, but we care most about what kind of men you become. A close-knit, small community where people know each other well and care about each other deeply is the best possible way to accomplish the goal of producing decent, humane, kind, and fully integrated human beings.

St. Stephen's has also bucked current trends and remained a single sex school. A school is not a good school merely because it is coed or because it is single sex. Certainly at this school, we believe in enrolling boys of diverse backgrounds, and since coeducation produces a kind of diversity that we exclude, I appreciate the argument that we are missing out on an opportunity. On the other hand, we've studied the issue carefully and believe that the current available information in the area of child and adolescent development, in the area of class dynamics, in the area of academic achievement, and in the area of character development, tells us that all-boy education offers unique opportunities. So we are proud of being a boys' school, and we will remain one.

Another fundamental core of our school is the tradition of high standards. We believe that hard work is important, and we ask you to stretch yourself academically. We believe that you are capable of being honorable, forthright, and decent, and so we expect it. We tolerate nothing less. We believe that you are capable of service to your community at a young age, and so we expect that, too, through our Saturday program, which is unique as far as I know among schools, and which is something that is a core part of our mission. We ask all these things of you because we believe that this kind of challenge will best *help you know yourself*, and in knowing yourself, you will be able to transcend yourself and serve a greater good more effectively.

Every year I tell you these things about your school because I want you to understand that our program is a purposeful, thoughtful undertaking. We do what we do because we have concluded, after long and careful examination and a certain amount of trial and error, that it is the most effective way to proceed, to accomplish our mission. Feel free to ask us "Why?" if you don't understand why we do what we do. Keep us on our toes. We ought to have good answers for you. If we don't, we need to go back to the drawing board. We want you to take ownership of St. Stephen's. It is your school. You can make it better by engaging it fully, by doing the best you can in every area, by caring deeply about the quality of life on our little campus.

My final point today goes to the heart of our mission. We are a church school. We are an Episcopal School. We are devoted to the life, ideals, and example of Jesus Christ. What this does *not* mean is as important as what it does mean. It does *not* mean that we have an exclusive grip on the truth. It does *not* mean that those who believe differently from us are wrong, or bad, or excluded from knowing God. It does *not* mean that our path to knowing God is the only path, or that people on other paths cannot have a relationship with God that is true and fulfilling.

It *does* mean that we take our religion seriously. It *does* mean that we believe Jesus Christ gave us a transcendent, beautiful, and difficult truth, a challenging path that is difficult to follow but can lead us to a greater understanding and into a relationship with God. It *does* mean that we believe your spiritual life is tremendously important and *has been one of the great forces in shaping the human story we call history.* We believe you need to take it seriously and consider it carefully. What path, we want you to ask, is the right path for you? If that happens to be the difficult path of following this remarkable man, Jesus Christ, and hearing his message of love, we believe that is a good thing.

And that is what we do believe, that Jesus Christ's central message was a message of love. God loves you. This central message informs everything we do. This love is not the sloppy sentimental love of Hollywood or soap operas or romance novels. It is not easy. In fact, it is a mystery. It is something we can only approach and never truly know. In this imperfect, fallen world of injustice, unfairness, and horrible, unexplainable tragedy, it ultimately involves a leap of faith. I do not pretend to have an answer to exactly what the love of God is, but the best path I've been able to find is that of that simple Nazarene, and frankly, other religious traditions say the same thing in different words. "Love your neighbor as yourself." "Love your enemy." None of us succeed in loving our neighbor as ourselves or loving our enemy. Sometimes we wonder if we even *want* to succeed.

You heard today the readings from Matthew, the Sermon on the Mount, about love. You heard also the reading from Corinthians, Chapter 13, about love being the greatest of the fundamental human qualities. You heard from a proverb of Solomon that "hatred stirreth up strifes: but love covereth all sins." You helped read a Psalm of David, which begins with a determined statement of aspiration, "I will love thee, O Lord, my strength." All these readings represent man's eternal struggle to understand God, to know Him and to know His love. These readings suggest you are not alone in this quest to understand your life and to understand God. The quest is passed from generation to generation. It is the shared condition of all thoughtful mortals that they wonder about the mystery of life and the mystery of God's love, and they humbly seek to pursue it the best way they know how.

Our school joins that ageless quest. We seek to know and love God, to love one another, to love our enemies. It is hard work, but it is noble work. We love you, and we invite you to join us in God's work.

Let us pray: "Almighty God, we beseech thee, with thy gracious favor, to behold our school, that knowledge may be increased among us, and all good learning flourish and abound. Bless all who teach and all who learn; and grant that in humility of heart, they may ever look unto thee, who art the fountain of all wisdom; through Jesus Christ our Lord. Amen."

MONDAY, SEPTEMBER 10—FIRST SENIOR CHAPEL TALK OF THE 2001-2002 ACADEMIC YEAR, DELIVERED BY JOEL KOHN

I drew the short straw, so here I am, the first senior speaker of the year. I think they rigged it, though. They wanted me to be first. They knew you'd listen to me, and they're right, you will. "Why?" you may be asking yourself? Well, it's quite obvious, really. First of all, I'm strikingly handsome, and you're naturally drawn to my good looks. I'm the Brad Pitt of St. Stephen's, so it's a lucky thing you're not girls or you might be rushing the podium. Second, I'm charmingly funny. See . . . you're laughing already. You like funny guys like me, which explains why I may simply be the most popular boy in school. Third, I'm smarter than you are. Just ask the teachers. You can see them all nodding in agreement. You guys have a tendency to listen to smart people, so of course you'll listen to a really, really smart guy like me. Fourth, I'm humble . . . Your laughter here really is a little inappropriate. Finally, you'll all agree that I'm different—some say weird, but I don't encourage that kind of talk. I'm the tree hugging, eco-loving, music-making, anti-jock. God, how I hate to sweat! But there's another part of my difference, in the context of St. Stephen's Episcopal School for young lads, that brings me to my central point today. Just like Jesus of Nazareth, I'm a Jew.

Now, I'm not the only Jew here at St. Stephen's. There is a surprisingly large number of us here—maybe thirty or forty. And then there are Shiite and Sunni Moslems, and Hindus and Buddhists. We are all welcomed here. That's a strength of this place. The rabbis come in pretty often. We've had mullahs and other holy men and women. Our Humanities course examines religion seriously, and we learn about the histories of various religions. We celebrate and recognize a wide variety of high holy days. All this is good, and before I begin to criticize St. Stephen's, which I am about to do, although I hope it will be in a constructive way, I want to make clear my love for this place so you do not misunderstand me.

This school has become a second home for me. The classes are interesting, the teachers are great, except, of course, for those like my advisor, Mr. Meader, who makes me exercise every day, even when I'm sick or tired, or sick *and* tired. At St. Stephen's, he's the resident sadist, and, of course, every school needs to have one, so I guess he fills a character-building role of sorts. If you'd like to join me in giving him a resounding "Boo," please feel free . . . Thank you all for you enthusiasm . . .

But, I digress . . . I do like this place, but I have a problem, and it's pretty fundamental. It's the cross, that thing on the altar behind me. The cross is on our school crest. It's on our walls. It's in the dining room. It's on our football helmets. It's everywhere. It bugs me. You might reasonably ask how I could go to a Christian school and not expect to see crosses all over the place. Good question. I don't have a good answer. But I have come to believe during my time here that this Christian school does not need the cross. As Ms. White said at the opening convocation, this school stands for the fundamental message of Jesus, which is a message of love. To me, the cross is not about love. Every time I see it, I think to myself, "What kind of a God would require his son to be tortured to death?" What would you think of a parent who would let that happen to his kid? The cross, to me, is about a horrible death, and who do many Christians believe killed Jesus? Us Jews, that's who. Just read the Gospel of John. Parts of it read like a pamphlet on anti-Semitism. We learned in ninth grade that that gospel was written seventy or so years after the death of Jesus. And it was written in Greek by a guy who probably didn't even speak Aramaic, which was the language of Jesus. And it was written in a time when Rome was looking for scapegoats and finding Jews to be a pretty easy target. It was the Romans who invented crucifixion, not the Jews, but never mind, you all know that.

I'm bothered by more than the fact that the cross was a pre-gas, pre-electricity, pre-guillotine symbol of Roman capital punishment. Instead, it is the centuries old tradition of the cross as a symbol of brutal oppression of my people that rankles me. The cross wasn't even important to Christians until Constantine saw it in the sky and thought of it as a sword for conquering everyone who differed from him. He used the cross as a way to consolidate his power, his control, his dominance. At the Council of Nicea, dissent within the Christian community was eliminated, and all Christians had to adopt one creed, the only creed, and it's still used today and followed. Constantine's cross politics made it blasphemy to think or worship in any way contrary to *his* way. This was the beginning of big trouble for us Jews.

I know I'm simplifying for the sake of time, and in order to make my point clear, and I know almost all of you know this stuff from our Humanities core. I also know I should apologize now if I am being offensive to any of you. I do not mean to be. I do not mean to "dis" all Christianity. I'm interested only in religions of a certain form that I will call literalist-fundamentalism, of which I believe the cross is emblematic. All religions have these people, by the way, not just Christianity. Look at the ultra-orthodox Jewish sects in Israel who advocate violence and believe it is either their way or you die. Look at the Ayatollah Khoumeni wannabes who keep women ignorant and under sheets and say right out in the open that Allah instructs them to kill the infidels. All our traditions seem to breed these radical folks. Every religion has its version of the KKK. These people suspend their brains and believe blindly. They lose sight of the fundamental message that their traditions teach. They narrow the ways to know God. They eliminate all paths but their own. And Christianity, sadly, behind the emblem of the crusaders' cross, has committed atrocities or allowed atrocities or created a climate that encouraged atrocities that make some of the awful acts of terrorists in the Middle East look small.

Consider the crusaders. More Jews were killed on the way to the Holy Land than were Moslem infidels *in* the Holy Land. Consider the pogroms of Russia. Consider Martin Luther's anti-Semitic diatribes. Consider the Holocaust itself and the Roman Catholic Church's seeming indifference. And all of this has been done with the cross leading the Christian flock.

So, to me and many other non-Christians, the cross is a symbol of death and oppression. It is hard for us to look at it without thinking of the dark side of all religion. It has little or nothing to do with the message of love that Jesus of Nazareth preached. In fact, it seems to be the absolute opposite.

You might now reasonably ask, what exactly am I trying to accomplish by saying all this from this St. Stephen's podium with the cross hanging behind me? I really have two goals, one reasonable and the other unlikely. The reasonable one first. I just hope to remind the Christian majority here that some people see things differently than you, and they have some good reasons. Your cross sends out many messages. Be sensitive to that, and you will understand others better.

My unlikely goal is to suggest that the Christian message of St. Stephen's is a worthy and admirable one. It is compatible with the messages of other humane and thoughtful people from other traditions. It is, I believe in my heart, too good for the symbol of the cross. Neither St. Stephen's nor good Christians anywhere need that symbol. They are too good for it. It is a symbol of triumphal arrogance and oppression. I would love to see this school take down the cross, or, at the very least, downplay it by placing the star of David and other religious symbols near it and on an equal footing. I would like to see us change our crest.

This will not happen, of course, but I would like it. I do love this school. I do want it to always strive to be better. I'm standing before you as a completely loyal and proud member of our school community. I am trying to love you, and I am trying to love God, and I hope this talk today will be taken in that spirit.

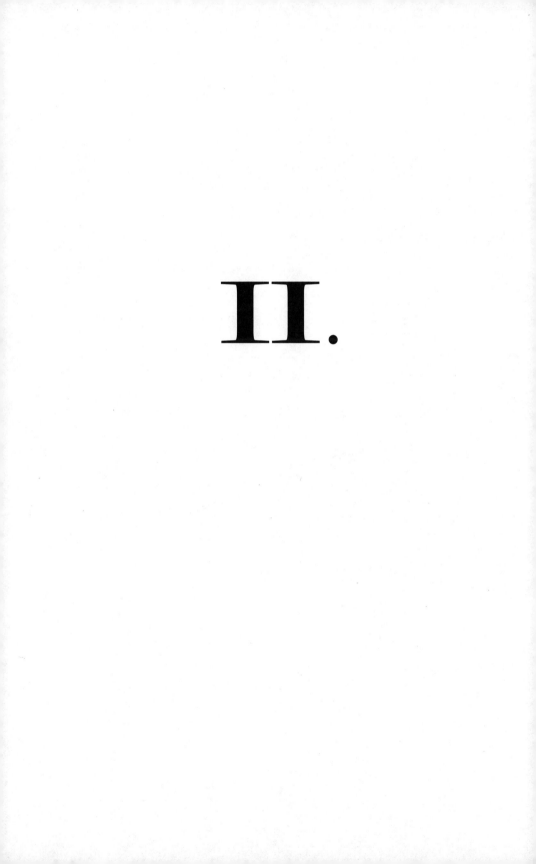

II.

Chapter 5

JOURNAL ENTRY: NIGHT, SEPTEMBER 11, 2001

I'm writing this in front of the TV, at home, where I'm watching Dan Rather talk. Mom and Steph are watching with me. My head's so full of stuff, I don't know what to say. There's too much, but at the same time, there's not enough. We see these pictures over and over, and the talks with people who are crying or hurt or just standing there like they're paralyzed are starting to smoosh together. The news people say the same thing over and over again, but every few minutes something new comes in, and it's usually pretty bad stuff. All this is the too-much part; I just cannot get a handle on it, like it's way bigger than me. The not-enough part is that nobody knows who or why, or if it will happen again. It would be nice to have some answers instead of just more questions. It would be nice to be certain about something out there.

Mom's been on the phone all night. When she's not on the phone, she's hugging me or Steph. She's doing lots of quiet crying—tears on her face but no sound. Her voice cracks when she talks. So far, no close friends of hers are missing, but she's taking this whole deal hard. I don't know what I feel. It almost seems fake, like it's a movie. This whole day wasn't real to me, and if I'm honest, I have to say I don't feel anything. I'm not scared. I'm not sad. I'm just like I am when I see a real bad traffic wreck on the evening news. I sort of think, "Wow, look at that. I'm sure glad I wasn't in the car." But that's about as much feeling as I get. Maybe if I knew somebody, it would be different, but as it is, it's just stuff happening inside the TV, like everything else that happens on TV.

School today was pretty far out. There we were, sitting in our Humanities course, which had started at 8:30, and it was getting just a few minutes from being over at 10:00 when the teacher, Ms. Marks, gets called out of the room. Ms. Marks comes back in just as the bell rings, and tells the other teacher, Mr. Randall, to go out. She tells us to stay where we are for a few minutes. When Mr. Randall comes back in, he's all red in the face, and he says we should stay where we are for just a minute, and he and Ms. Marks go back out in the hall. Things are a little fishy, and we're all talking to each other, wondering what's up. When they came back into class, it was already well past 10:00 and we got quiet right away.

Ms. Marks stood in front of us and said in a real quiet, serious voice, "We're sorry, boys, to keep you waiting. We just learned of some serious events that happened in New York City and Washington. All of you should report immediately to your advisor's office. Please go there now."

That's what we did. Joel Kohn and a couple others were already in Mr. Meader's office when I got there. Mr. Meader had cleared off his couch and had unfolded some of the chairs he leans in the corner. I sat on the couch next to Joel. "Hi, Jake," he said. "We'll wait for the others to get here before we talk."

So we sat there in quiet for about five minutes, and then we were all together. Mr. Meader said, "We will go to the chapel at 11:00, but let me tell you what I know. First, I don't know much. I do know that a plane crashed into one of the two World Trade Center towers early this morning shortly after you went into class. A second plane crashed into the other World Trade Center a little later. Then a third plane crashed into the Pentagon outside Washington. Just a few minutes ago, a fourth plane crashed outside of Pittsburgh. Also, just a few minutes ago, one of the World Trade Center towers collapsed. That is everything I know. Now, we have a few minutes before chapel. Let's see if we can't get each of you on the phone with one of your parents for a quick conversation. Do the following"—and then he read from a little typed sheet—"One, find out how they are; two, tell them how you are; three, tell them you are going to chapel at 11:00; four, tell them you will call them back right after chapel; five, tell them you have to get off the phone to let others use it."

So that's what we did. I reached Mom at work, and did what Mr. Meader said to do. Mom was speaking real soft—I could barely hear her. She thanked me for calling and said she was going to get Steph at school. She was going to wait to hear more from me, and I should call her at home. All of us got through to our parents except for one guy whose father was in New York on business, and his mother's phone was busy. He was pretty freaked, and I can't blame him.

Chapel was sort of spooky. The place was completely silent except for feet hitting the stone floor as we went to our seats. When we were all seated, Ms. White comes in the back, and she walks the entire length of the chapel in complete silence except the clack-clack of her shoes. When she gets to the front, she turns and says, "Let us sing together our school hymn, 'O God Our Help in Ages Past.'" So we did.

When we sit down, she starts to speak. She says we are undergoing a national emergency, that we are enduring a terrible tragedy. Then she walks us through everything that happened, plus she adds that another tower has collapsed. When she's done giving us the facts, she gives us some advice. She tells us to love one another, to love our families, and to appreciate our good fortune in most areas of our life. She tells us to reserve judgment. "Don't leap to conclusions," she says, "You are young and don't need to have all the answers." She advised us not to believe everything we hear, to use our common sense and critical thinking skills. She tells us to be very careful not to condemn any group of people merely because of the acts of some individuals. Finally, she tells us "the best way to help yourself is to help others." Some of us will learn in the days ahead that people close to us have died, and we need to support one another. Then she says, "Let us pray," and we say the Lord's Prayer.

Just before we depart, she says that we should continue to try to reach our parents, that anyone who wants to leave school today may do so with their parents only and with the knowledge and consent of their advisors, that lunch will be served at 12:30 p.m., and that televisions have been set up in the forum rooms and in the common room. The gym will be open after lunch for those who want to get some exercise, but boys must be either with their advisor or in a spot known to their advisor until their parents pick them up at the end of the day, which will be at 4:00 p.m. since all formal athletic practices are cancelled.

I reach Mom, and she decides to come get me at 2:00 p.m. So I eat lunch, talk to Mr. Meader and Joel, and watch the tube. A few minutes before I leave, the word gets out that school will start one hour late tomorrow—at 9:00—with a longer than usual chapel service and that parents are welcome.

What a day!

JOURNAL ENTRY: NIGHT, SEPTEMBER 12, 2001

You might think there would be no homework given what's going down, but you'd be wrong. They don't just give us homework. They give us more than I ever had in my life. It's like they don't want us doing anything else. I'm watching the eleven o'clock news, which is my break, and then I've got another hour or more of homework. What's with this school?!

The only thing worth mentioning today was the chapel service. Mom and Steph came, along with a ton of other parents. The back of the place was packed. So was the balcony. Some people had to stand. The service was similar to the start of school but without the senior ceremony stuff. Also, there was a rabbi there along with a Muslim priest, or whatever you call him, and they walked in with our chaplain. All three of them spoke briefly about how their religions condemn violence and how we all worship the same God. Then Ms. White spoke for a little longer, and she basically told us that our job was to do our jobs really well. She said that we are students and should be expected at a time like this to be the best students we know how to be, and at St. Stephen's, that means more than doing work. It means listening and learning and paying attention to the world around us. It means caring about each other.

Well, if she wants us to do all that, she should have the teachers give us less work. After chapel, it was back to classes and the adjusted regular schedule. Tomorrow, the school day will be regular.

Baltimore Sun Headlines, September 12, 2001
DEVASTATION
Hijacked Planes Destroy World Trade Center Towers
Third Jetliner Slams Into Pentagon

Jake

We gather here today as a school community to pray, to reflect, to ask for help, to remember those who have died, and to draw strength from one another. In the blink of an eye, our world has changed. Our lives are changed. But events have unfolded too quickly for us to even understand the facts, let alone comprehend how our lives have changed. We are stunned in a way that only those who lived through Pearl Harbor can remember. What does one do at such a moment? How are we to behave?

We can start by recognizing and embracing some of the natural feelings that sweep over us. Some of you, like me, may be over-whelmed with the fragility of the human condition. Life seems more precious today. Hold hard to that truth. Fill your lives with the things you value most. Gather around you those whom you love. Value the acute sense of togetherness tragedy can prompt. Take seriously every precious moment—*carpe diem, tempus fugit.*

But some of the feelings that wash over us are less welcome. You, like me, may feel fear. We are afraid for our country, for our fellow cit-izens, for our parents, for our children, and for ourselves. But mostly we are afraid of the unknown. None of us likes uncertainty. The dark scares us because it obscures objects, which then become mysterious. We like dawn because it throws light on a subject. It gives us under-standing. Sadly, at times of fear, prompted by the unknown, by our ignorance, by being in the dark, we are likely to act in ways that later make us ashamed. Most bigotry and intolerance stems from fear, from ignorance. At this time, we must guard against our fear leading us down paths that we will come to regret. The three great Western faiths are represented in this chapel today, which is symbolic of our shared rejection of fear and ignorance. We join together from many traditions to affirm the human family, to join in rejecting fear and terror. We should draw strength from one another in refusing to allow the terrorist to win by imitating his character, which is one of ignorance, hate, and fear. Do not let the terrorist win by allowing fear to cloud your life. Let us strive to be brave together.

Some of you, like me, are wondering how we can help, and right now we feel helpless. We want something to do. We want to be useful, perhaps to rush up to New York City. It just doesn't seem right to be standing by as spectators. This school will do some small part to help. We are already considering options, and we will ask for your input. But there is one thing we all can do right now. We can simply go about our daily lives as effectively and courageously as we know how. We should go about the business of living fully and engaging entirely in the business of our lives. For you, be good students. Not only work hard in your classes, but pay attention to events around you in the school, the community, the country. Work hard to become a contributing, informed citizen. Care about each other. Support your fellow students. If you do these things, you will become the sort of service-oriented, well-prepared, thoughtful citizens our country will need to face whatever challenges belong to tomorrow.

While we are living our full lives, we should hesitate before rushing to judgment. Listen carefully. Listen to our leaders, to thoughtful commentators. Remember that, in our pluralist society, people of good faith can and should argue forcefully for different courses of action. *Don't believe in a world of purely good versus purely evil.* Be attuned to the grays of most issues. We are being launched into a complicated new world fraught with nuance and complexity. Assume your thoughtful perspectives in humility, respectful of those who see things differently, yet willing to insist upon standards of decency and civility and kindness.

Let me conclude by sharing some tentative good news. A long night of working phones and e-mail seems to have confirmed that our school family of students, their parents, faculty, staff, their immediate families, and our alumni have escaped death at the hands of the terrorists who have attacked us. I cannot begin to express adequately my immense relief and gratitude for this little community's good fortune.

Let us pray:

"Almighty God, who has given us this good land for our heritage, we humbly beseech thee that we may always prove ourselves a people mindful of thy favor and glad to do thy will. Bless our land with honorable industry, sound learning, and pure manners. Save us from violence, discord, and confusion; from pride and arrogance; and from every evil way. Defend our liberties, and fashion into one united people the multitudes brought hither out of many kindreds and tongues. Endow with the spirit of wisdom those to whom, in thy name, we entrust the authority of government, that there may be justice and peace at home, and that, through obedience to thy law, we may put forth thy praise among the nations of the earth. In this time of prosperity, fill our hearts with thankfulness, and in the day of trouble, do not allow our trust in thee to fail; all which we ask through Jesus Christ our Lord. Amen.

Baltimore Sun Headlines, September 13, 2001
Tracking the Terrorists
Clues Are Scarce; Survivors Few in N.Y. Rubble

JOURNAL ENTRY: NIGHT, SEPTEMBER 13, 2001

Too much damn work. It's eleven o'clock-news time again, and I've got more to do than I can get done tonight. We read the newspaper together in Humanities. I didn't pay much attention when the USS Cole blew up, and I'd never even heard of the '96 Khobar Towers stuff. This guy bin Laden has been trying to fuck us up for a while. President Bush says we're going to hunt him down and punish him, and Colin Powell says we're at war. There are more than 5,000 people dead. The pictures in the paper are pretty awful, and the TV shots of the towers I'm looking at right now are unreal. This is getting scarier to me than it was at first. Rumsfeld says this thing is going to last a long time. Some kid asked today if we could be drafted. Ms. Marks said it was possible that a draft could be put back into effect by Congress if it was necessary. Being a soldier is just about the farthest thing I can imagine ever having to do. This is getting to be a little too real.

Maybe I'll just hit the sack and blow off the rest of my homework. All things considered, it doesn't seem very important.

Baltimore Sun Headlines, September 14, 2001
U.S. Pledges 'Global Assault';
Warns of More Terror Attacks
Death Toll of 5,000--bin Laden Labeled Suspect

JOURNAL ENTRY: NIGHT, SEPTEMBER 14, 2001

We watched the National Prayer Service in Washington from a big screen set up in the school theatre today. All these past presidents were there and Al Gore, too. Every kind of religious leader spoke, and this old guy, Billy Graham, spoke, too. It was some really heavy shit when they sang "The Battle Hymn of the Republic." People were all choked up—you could tell.

President Bush says that we're peaceful most of the time, but when we're angry we kick ass, or words not too far from that. He says we'll end this thing the way we want it ended. He visited New York today. I'm watching that on the tube now. The President has got a ton of stuff to worry about. I wouldn't want to be in his shoes. It's good, I guess, he has his dad around. They looked pretty close at the prayer service. I think his father's proud of him.

Mom's been staying off my back, which is good. She's quiet. Steph's been less of a pain, too. I get to sleep tonight. Finally! I stayed up until two last night. I sure wish I didn't have to get up for the community service stuff tomorrow, but I have to admit, with all this shit going down, it's hard to feel too sorry for myself.

Baltimore Sun Headlines, September 15, 2001
Call Up of 50,000 Troops OK'd
Congress Endorses the Use of Force
Lawmakers Approve $40 Billion for Relief, Military Response
More Than 100 Sought in Probe

Baltimore Sun Headline, September 16, 2001
'We're At War,' Bush Warns

JOURNAL ENTRY: NIGHT, SEPTEMBER 16, 2001

On my only day off, Mom drags me to church. I'm way past pissed off. I wanted to sleep in today, but no-o-o-o! We have to go pray. I go to church every goddamn day. Mom says she needs us to be together, to go to church as a family. Fine, what about what I need, like some sleep? We get back, and I eat lunch and crash in front of the TV news. There's not even any football on to zone out in front of. I get up at about 5:00, and I do school work until 10:00. This has been one sucky day of "rest," let me tell you that.

Yesterday sucked too just because we were at school, not doing what we want to do. But I have to admit; Joel could make cleaning a toilet bowl fun. We learned how to test water from some guy who works for the Chesapeake Bay Foundation, and we took a bunch of samples. Then we picked up some trash and went home.

At home, I got Mom to agree to let me get my learner's permit. I read the pamphlet already and the test is supposed to be real easy. They give Driver's Ed at school on Saturday afternoons, so I can do that then. Then I can practice driving around with Mom on Sundays. I need to get my license. A lot of my classmates already got theirs. I'm late.

Baltimore Sun Headlines, September 17-23
Taliban Face Ultimatum
Warning: Give Up bin Laden or Feel the Full Wrath of U.S.
Markets Reopen, Then Tumble
Take bin Laden Dead or Alive, President Says
U.S. Shifts Focus to Recovery
Bush Orders Planes to Gulf, Will Speak to Nation Tonight
Bush Braces Nation for Battle
New Estimate of Missing in N.Y. is 6,333
Congress OKs $15 Billion to Rescue Airline Industry
Taliban Refuse U.S. Demand
Taliban Lose Key Arab Support

Jake

Mom backed off the church stuff today when I threw a major fit. Thank God! This week was a bummer. The work at this school just gets worse and worse. When are we supposed to sleep? My school rule has always been to do well enough so they'll leave me alone. That doesn't fly here. First, it's not easy to do well. Second, the classes are so small they notice everything. You can't slide by.

The adults in school are completely obsessed by the stuff going on. Mr. Meader talks about it in advisory, at lunch, and every time I see him. Humanities class starts off with a review of the newspaper every day. I got to admit I was a little surprised by an article that a guy named Friedman wrote in the *Sun*. He claims to be some sort of Middle East expert and writes that "the Arab world is split 50-50 between those appalled by the bombing and those applauding it." Shit! If he's right, we got problems.

Two chapel talks were hard to ignore. One young teacher, who just got out of college and is a major league history type, said we need to understand why all these people hate us and that our own policies caused the bombings. We should not meet violence with violence. We should not seek revenge. We should look for understanding. We have no one to blame but ourselves, he said.

The very next day an old guy on the faculty, who's been hanging around this place his whole life, said he respected everyone's right to have an opinion, but that this country has a right to defend itself. He says that whether our past policies were wise, or just, or not was a matter where reasonable people can disagree. But unwise policy does not justify murder of innocent civilians. He said it was foolishness to think bin Laden is after some sort of policy change. Bin Laden hates us because we represent pluralism and individual freedom, and that scares him. He hates that sort of freedom. He wants to wipe us off the face of the earth. We are the devil, who he hates the same way Hitler hated Jews or the way the KKK hates black people. Don't be naive, he said. It's a really nasty world out there. There are people who want to hurt us, and they will hurt us if we let them. We must be strong enough to do those things necessary to beat the Hitlers and the KKK's and the bin Ladens of the world, or they will beat us. It will be hard, and it will be unpleasant, and some of us will die, but we must do it.

It's sort of cool having the teachers disagreeing right in front of us. They were polite, but they were real serious. I'm not sure a whole lot more needs to be said. People are just going around in a circle.

On Saturday, Joel and I set up a net to see what bug life is in the water just below this place called Lake Roland. There was a lot of stuff. I could identify some of it for him as we were putting nymphs in these little tubes. They're the same stuff trout eat. Then we set up another net down by Howard Street, but there was nothing—zero. Joel says the river dies completely somewhere below the lake. Pretty interesting. We did see a great blue heron right by the expressway. He must be lost or dumb!

I passed the written part of the driving test Saturday afternoon. It was easy. Afterward, Mom took me driving for two hours out on country roads. It was way cool, but she was grumpy the whole time. She just sat there like some kind of zombie. Every once in a while, she'd say "slow down," or "put on your blinker," or "stay on your side of the road." But that's it. What's with her?!

I have about three hours of schoolwork to do, and then I'm gonna crash at about 10:00. There's too much of everything in my life these days except sleep.

Chapter 6

Baltimore Sun Headlines, September 24-30

U.S. Plans Pakistan's Role

Taliban Officials Say They Cannot Locate Terrorist bin Laden

U.S. Freezes bin Laden Assets

Tornado Kills Two UM Students

Afghans Urged to Defy Taliban

Pakistan Warning Taliban

Bush Wants U.S. Back in the Air

President Says It's Safe to Fly

U.S. in Hot Pursuit of Terrorists

Retaliation Will Come, Bush Vows

JOURNAL ENTRY: SUNDAY, SEPTEMBER 30, 2001

Mr. Meader pulled me aside at the start of the week and asked how I was doing. I said, "Good," but he said he was worried. He said that advisors always checked up on students after two full weeks of class, and that my teachers are worried that I'm a little disorganized, that I don't know how to distinguish the important stuff from the little stuff. He says that he sees some of that in Geometry.

I'm real good in math, though, so I don't see how he can complain much. He also said I look tired. My soccer coach told him I was a little dragged out on the field, which is true, but I'm not gonna admit that to anyone.

Then Mr. Meader suggests I go see one of the Study Skills specialists. No way, man! I'm not one of the dumb kids they send to some learning center, like in the county. They're a bunch of retards. He said he thought he'd call home to check in with Mom, but I did my best possible ass-kissing routine and got him to back off. I told him that Mom was way stressed with her new job and that she didn't need to worry about me because I'm fine. I told him that I was getting the hang of things. He listened to me and said, "OK." But he also said he was gonna see how things went this week.

And things went as usual. It took past eleven every night to get all this frigging work done. Here I am now, and it's already past nine on Sunday night, and I'm finishing up a stupid paper on the Euro for Humanities, which is due tomorrow. Thank God I found a great website hooked into the University of Maryland. They've got all this research done on the Euro with all the footnotes and stuff already there. It's gonna cut my work about in half. I guess the students got together down there and published their papers just to save each other trouble. Between this stupid journal, a major Physics assignment, and enough French vocabulary to choke a chicken, I wouldn't go to bed at all tonight if it weren't for this website.

Beyond working my ass off, it was a pretty uneventful week. I'm getting the hang of the school routine. It's not as complicated as it seemed at first. The chapels are pretty harmless for the most part. I just zone out and look around if it's boring. It's actually pretty relaxing. The organ music isn't too bad, and those colored windows have something different in them every time I check them out. One of the seniors gave a talk on a scuba diving accident where he got something called "the bends" and nearly died. That was cool. The food in the refectory is good. That's one strange thing—I never heard of good school food before. I pretty much pig out and listen to Joel give Mr. Meader crap about one thing or another.

Saturday morning was better than I expected. Mr. Meader drove us in the school van out Falls Road and past Lake Roland. We took water samples and checked out the bugs under rocks from downstream of where an old factory used to be, all the way under the Jones Fall Expressway and up to these old stone buildings where the river dips back under Falls Road. The stream is just dead from the old factory and below. But above the factory are all sorts of bug life. I'll be interested to see what the water samples say when we get them back from the lab.

Right near the end of our walk upstream, an old blue heron, which we watched standing real still, suddenly stabbed down into the water and came up with a fish. He gulped that sucker down in about two swallows. Then he saw us and gave this low, hollow croak and took off. He only flew about two feet off the water, all stretched out straight like an arrow, and he took a big squirt of a dump right in the river before veering up into a tree. I'd never seen one of those guys up in a tree before. I thought they just hung out on the ground. Pretty weird—tall stringy bird like that perched up in a tree. You wonder how they decide where to fish and when to get off the water.

Last week I saw one idiot heron acting like a fisherman in a part of the river that isn't much better than a concrete culvert. He's gotta be hungry. This one at least found some fish. I don't know whether it was a trout or not. The water's right on the edge of being cold enough. We measured it—62° F in a shady deep spot, so it could have been a trout. I'm betting on a fall fish, but my guess is that the heron doesn't give a rat's ass. To him, a fish is a fish is a fish. Comical birds. I guess it's good they can hang out in trees, because I'm sure they can't swim, and I'll bet they can't run fast on those skinny stick legs. They'd be vulnerable to just about anything that wanted to eat them if they had to nest or hang out on the ground. I wonder who a heron's natural enemy is. I'll have to ask Joel.

Next time we go to that stretch of water, I'm bringing a rod just to see if I can stir up any action.

Mom said we had to do the family church thing again today, so we did. There was too much work for me to get down to the Gunpowder this afternoon, but I did ride my dirt bike for an hour just to clear my head from French vocab.

All the adults at school, at church, in the newspaper, and Mom at home can't think about anything but Afghanistan. Some of the kids at school think about it, too, and you hear discussions at lunch or in the hallways. But the whole thing seems far away. Everybody's got flags on their houses. There are flag decals on cars, and people fly flags on poles from their car windows, which makes them get real frayed and tattered at the ends. It's hard for me to relate to all this. I guess I feel a little guilty about not feeling much. I didn't know those people who got killed, and I didn't know the firefighters and policemen who died, so it isn't personal for me. I've been to New York, but I never paid much attention to those towers. At school, the seniors all gave blood along with the faculty. The rest of us are too young. A bunch of kids went up to New York, and some went down to look over the Pentagon last weekend. I think they're mostly curious, but it would probably be better if they stayed out of the way. It's hard for me to know what the right thing to do or feel is. I guess it's good that the teachers disagree, that people seem to have a bunch of different ways of looking at it. It's like it's OK to be confused about how to feel.

Jake

I got to stop writing and get back to work. Work. That's what this school is all about. I don't know why I let myself get suckered into it. It's like some invisible hand that's grabbed me and pulled me in. School was never work before. You just did a bunch of stuff that was pretty boring and pretty easy and nobody cared or paid much attention. The dumb kids got a lot of attention and so did the delinquents, but the rest of us could get by pretty easy. Everybody works at St. Stephen's. It's just sorta what you do. Nobody makes a particularly big deal out of it, but the teachers just expect it and the students just do it. It's like there's a work drug or something that oozes out of the bricks of the place. I don't want to work this hard, but it's hard to imagine not doing the work. Plus, I don't want to be one of the dumb guys. Maybe they've just brainwashed me already, and I've become one of them without even knowing it. Whatever . . . I got to get to work.

Chapter 7

Baltimore Sun Headlines, October 1-7
Bin Laden Under Taliban Guard
Bush OKs Some Flights at National
Rumsfeld Heads to the Gulf
U.S. Has Proof on bin Laden, NATO Says
$75 Billion Sought to Jolt Economy
U.S. Plans Millions in Afghan Aid
Bonds Hits 71st Home Run
Spend Less, Cut Taxes, Bush Says
Final Salute to Ripken
Time's Short, Bush Warns the Taliban

OCTOBER 4, 2001—LETTER FROM RECTOR
MARY WHITE TO MS. KAREN COLLINS

Dear Karen:

Thank you very much for your understanding and cooperation over the past two days as we've worked to reach an appropriate conclusion regarding Jake's poor decision. It is always much easier to help a boy when the school and the parent speak with one voice. Even at our first meeting, when the possibility of expulsion remained very real, you supported without reservation the principle that academic honesty is important. It took particular courage for you to say that you would support whatever action we decided upon. Many parents have difficulty honoring in practice what they preach in principle, and you have given Jake a great gift by standing by your principles even when it hurts.

I am sure that we are in accord about the events of the last week, but the years have taught me that it is dangerous to assume anything when more than two or three people are involved. I am setting forth in this letter the facts and conclusions reached during our meetings in the hope that you will let me know immediately if there is some area where I am unclear or incorrect.

We have all agreed that Jake plagiarized when writing the Humanities paper he turned in on Monday. Jake freely admitted the fact to Ms. Marks and to Mr. Meader. We also agreed that Jake understood the rules against plagiarism, and he was completely open in admitting that he knew plagiarism was not only wrong but against specific school rules. When we pressed Jake for an explanation, he said he was "really busy, really rushed, and really stupid." You may recall his repeated words, "I just didn't think." That for me is the crux of the matter, and it is a fairly typical problem. It is entirely likely and entirely ordinary that Jake's actions were thoughtless. If he had been thinking, he would not have acted as he did. I am entirely persuaded that Jake's plagiarism was a hasty, unpremeditated, thoughtless act of an overwhelmed boy.

Nonetheless, he *should* "think." He is responsible for his actions and must be held accountable. We have chosen not to make this a matter for the Honor Committee and not to impose a disciplinary sanction because we believe that doing so would not be in the best interests of either the school or Jake. Since this was a thoughtless mistake as opposed to a premeditated deception, we believe it consistent with the school honor code to pursue the matter further through counseling and other informal remedial steps. This incident will be kept confidential, but any further dishonesty of any kind by Jake will cause this matter to be placed before the Honor Committee to give context to a subsequent violation. As we all understand, another honor infraction would make it unlikely that Jake would be able to remain at St. Stephen's.

We decided on the following cause of action: First, Jake needs to meet regularly with our Study Skills coordinator. Jake is more than bright enough to do the work here, but it's a new experience for him. I believe he will benefit from some tutoring in this area. Second, on Saturdays, after community service, Jake will meet with several people to talk about honor and the concept of honor. I believe he will find these conversations useful. Third, Jake will meet with me on several occasions during the coming months.

On the bright side, I believe Jake's poor judgment is an aberration. This incident must be treated as an opportunity not only to get his attention but also to influence his life. All of us working together will be able to persuade Jake of the fundamental importance of honorable behavior. Jake stated clearly that he wants to be here at St. Stephen's, and that should provide him with the motivation to take seriously the school's principles and standards.

Again, thank you for your help and understanding. Please call me if you have any questions or concerns.

Sincerely,
Mary White
Rector, St. Stephen's Episcopal School

Jake

Karen,

Do not be disheartened. Even our finest boys make mistakes. Do not assume that you have done anything wrong to cause this to happen, and do not conclude that Jake is suffering from an unremediable character flaw. As parents, we often find it hard to separate ourselves from our children, and we feel their pain as if it is our own. Go easy on him. I believe we have his full attention. He is embarrassed and ashamed. He needs your support and unconditional love. We will offer the same from our end along with a program designed to make this mistake a learning opportunity.

Warm regards,
Mary

October 4, 2001—Letter from Rector Mary White to Jake Phillips

Dear Jake:

We've spent a significant amount of time with one another over the past few days, and I imagine that you are still sorting out the many thoughts going through your head. First of all, let me say that I am glad indeed that you desire to stay at St. Stephen's. We want you here. Second, you should know that your candid, open reaction to being confronted with your honor mistake reflects well upon your character. Third, I do not believe you are a dishonest boy. On the other hand, you did act thoughtlessly. That thoughtlessness led to a dishonorable act. When it happens once, under some circumstances, it can be written off as a mere mistake—a serious mistake, but only a mistake—and not as a character flaw.

How you react now to the mistake you have made will shape you character in significant ways. Will you be able to look a mistake in the eye, take full ownership of it, resolve not to repeat it, and then take those actions necessary to transform your resolve into reality? If the answer is "yes," then you are on your way to becoming a young man of sound character. That is a large part of our mission at St. Stephen's.

We have laid out for you an educational and counseling program that we believe will help you learn and grow from your mistake. You have the information. I look forward very much to working with you, and I believe that you will become a stronger, more thoughtful young man from this experience. Please do not hesitate to drop by if you have questions or concerns, or if you just want to chat.

Sincerely,
Mary White
Rector, St. Stephen's Episcopal School

JOURNAL ENTRY: NIGHT, OCTOBER 7, 2001

The week from hell! I turned in my Humanities project on Monday, and Tuesday morning I was called into Ms. Marks' office. She asked me to sit down and said, "Jake, I'm concerned that the paper you turned in to me is not your own work and that you have not properly attributed its contents to the original sources. This is serious, and before you answer me, I want you to review in your mind the definition of plagiarism and whether you have transgressed."

I did what she said and just sat there for a moment, not really getting what she was talking about. Then I realized that my paper was all from the web site. It wasn't word for word or anything, but I used all

the good stuff from one of the papers I saw. It seemed to pull together all that other stuff I read. So I said, "I got a lot of my thoughts from
one place on the net, and I used them."

We sat for a second or two in total silence, and I was starting to
freak a little bit. There's no question, now that I had time to think
about it, that I broke the honor rule in the handbook. Hell, between
Mom, Ms. White, Mr. Meader, and Joel, I'd heard that stuff about a
jillion times. But it wasn't one of those things I paid much attention
to. You know, like background noise. You just don't think about stuff
like that. It didn't seem like a big deal when I was doing the paper. I
was just rushed, and this was way easier and faster than any other way
I could have done it. I just thought, "Cool, I can get this project out
of the way fast." The stuff is right there on the Net for anybody to use
for free, so I used it without giving it a second thought. Looking back,
that sounds pretty lame.

Ms. Marks asked, "Why, Jake? Why did you use it? Didn't you
know it was an honor violation?"

So I told her straight out that I didn't think about it at all. I just
did it. And, yeah, I would've known it was an honor violation if I'd
given it any thought. But I didn't.

She just looked at me. "Do you understand now that you've violated our Honor Code?"

"Yes," I said.

"Do you understand that an Honor Code violation can lead to
expulsion?"

"Yes," I said again, but inside I was starting to feel really lousy,
really bummed. I hadn't meant for this to happen. It wasn't like I went
out to fool anybody or anything. It was just stupid. I was just stupid,
and I don't think you should be expelled for being stupid unless you've
got a long record of being stupid.

Again, she's silent for awhile, and then she finally said, "Let's go see Mr. Meader."

Down the hall we went, knocked on his door, and went in. We sat down, and Ms. Marks told me to tell him what's up. So I did. He listened really carefully without even moving his hands. He looked right in my eyes the whole time, even for about half a minute after I finished.

Then he sighed, and pushed himself back in his chair and said, "Jake, Jake, Jake . . ." over and over again, and then he leaned forward and put his head in his hands and rubbed his whole face real hard, "What were you thinking?"

"I wasn't," I said, and that's the truth, but he knew and I knew that we had talked about this stuff. And sure enough, he said, "Even after our talks?"

I could see he was real disappointed in me, and for some reason it made me feel like crying. "Dumb," I said. "Dumb because it just didn't cross my mind, and I know it should have and . . ."

Then I did start to cry, and I couldn't talk, and I just sat there feeling like a stupid asshole crybaby who'd sold out Mr. Meader. When I got control of myself, I just said, "Sorry," and I sat there sniffling. Mr. Meader handed me some tissues, and I wiped my nose.

Then Mr. Meader said, "Ms. Marks and I need to talk. You go to class, and we'll decide what the next step is. Jake, you need to brace yourself. An honor violation here leads to serious consequences, including expulsion. You know what the handbook says about that. But we'll talk, and then we'll seek advice from Ms. White. She'll probably want to speak to you."

So I got up and left the room feeling lower than a worm. I had trouble concentrating in class, and I zoned out for most of the rest of the morning. At lunch, Mr. Meader told me that Ms. White wanted to see me during my free period at 1:10, so I went to the rector's office and the secretary there led me into Ms. White's private office. Ms. White asked me to sit down in one of the chairs in front of her desk, and then she came around from behind and sat down in the other chair. She asked the secretary to please close her door on the way out. I was so nervous I was almost shaking. My hands felt sticky and prickly, and my stomach had a lump, like a big hot meatball was sitting right in the middle of it. My throat was hot and tight as if I'd held my breath too long and needed air. It was a bummer of a feeling. We sat there quietly for a moment. She got up and went to a table in the corner and poured some water from a pitcher into a glass. She handed me the glass, and I choked it down. "Thanks," I said, and she just nodded.

"I have one question for you, Jake, and I want you to give it some thought before you answer. Do you want to be here at St. Stephen's?"

Almost before she'd finished and without any kind of thought, I surprised myself by blurting out, "Yes, yes I do."

Until that moment, I could not have guessed what my answer would be, and I kinda thought I'd say the opposite, but there it popped out of me, and I realized, in that very instant, it was true, but I wasn't sure why. The place is too hard. I've got like no life but school. I work every day. It seems like I work *all* day. I'm not doing that well. The Saturday requirement sucks. The dress code sucks. And I can give you a ton of other reasons to hate the place. But I wanted to stay, and I do want to stay, and wouldn't you know, that's what the next question was.

"Why?" she asked. "Why do you want to stay at St. Stephen's?"

This time I thought for a moment, but I wasn't sure, so I said so. "I don't know, Ms. White. This place is hard for me, and school's never been hard before. I'm tired most of the time, and I miss just hanging out and doing nothing on the weekends."

Then I tried to explain what I wasn't sure of myself—that the place made me want to be a part of it partly because of all the hard stuff and maybe because everybody was doing it together. I told her that it was the first time I'd really known any of my teachers, that I liked that the eleventh and twelfth graders were so into the place and weren't all hung up on themselves that they wouldn't talk to a new student like me. It hit me then, and I said it to her, that nobody at my old school would've even noticed that I'd plagiarized. They notice stuff at St. Stephen's—little and big stuff. It drives you crazy sometimes, but they're definitely paying attention. "They notice when my tie is down," I said, "or I haven't written enough, or if I look tired or unhappy, or if I score a goal in soccer, or if I get a couple of bad quiz grades in a row, and they say something to me about it. It's a pain, sometimes, but it's good, too."

Her eyes never left me the whole time I talked, and then she said, "I'm glad to know you want to be here, Jake, and I think you state your reasons well. They're good reasons. The obvious question now is, "Why did you act in this way when you knew it could cause you to leave St. Stephen's?"

So I went through my explanation, which sounded even lamer this time around, and she just watched me and listened quietly the whole time.

"Jake," she said when I was done, "you must think. Thoughtless acts can do as much harm as purposeful acts. Mr. Meader believes your explanation. So does Ms. Marks. So do I. But this sort of thoughtlessness is just not acceptable. Your mother is coming in at the end of the athletic period, and we will discuss at that time the matter of an appropriate school response. There will be a response designed to educate you and to promote the ideals of the school . . ."

I didn't hear much of the rest because the thought of Mom coming in to hear about this made the water-works start up again. I was wiping my face with the back of my hand and sniffling while she talked. She gave me time to get my act together, and then I went back to class. But I couldn't get my act together. The rest of the day was a total waste.

When I walked into Ms. White's office that evening, Mom was already there. She got up and gave me a hug and then sat back down on the tan couch underneath a big oil painting of the school's main building. I sat in a high-backed blue chair next to her. Ms. White sat across a low table, with the school history book on it. She was in another high-backed blue chair.

"Jake," she began, "your mother and I have had a good talk, but I think it is important for you to tell her in your own words what you did, your explanation for your actions, and your current thinking on the matter."

So that's what I did. Mom and Ms. White never took their eyes off me. I said the same things I said before, and I said I felt stupid, and I said I wanted to stay at St. Stephen's, and then I stopped.

Mom looked at me hard, but I could tell she was trying to control her feelings. She said real slow and soft, "You and I both know that you've made a serious mistake. You've been dishonest. Even if you didn't think before you acted, the result is the same. I don't know yet what the school will decide to do, but we both knew what we were getting into at St. Stephen's. The rules are clear. And you must accept the consequences of your actions, take responsibility for your mistake."

Then she turned toward Ms. White and said, "I will, of course, support completely any decision St. Stephen's makes. I do want you to know that I am hopeful that you will choose to let Jake stay here at school. I believe that he is basically honest, that his thoughtlessness is more of an issue at this point than is his honesty. I believe that he can learn from this experience and grow from it and perhaps make a contribution to St. Stephen's."

Ms. White smiled and nodded at Mom. "Thank you, Karen, for your support and for your understanding. I recognize how disappointed and hurt you are right now. I will not make a decision this evening about the next step. This matter could go to Honor Council. I could take disciplinary action myself or fashion some other appropriate response. But it is almost always prudent, I have found, to sleep on a hard problem, to consult with others carefully, and to see if a new day offers any fresh perspectives. Is there a time during which you are free tomorrow, at lunch hour perhaps?"

And so we were going to meet again on Wednesday. We rode home in complete silence. I drove, and Mom stared out the side window. When we got home, Stephanie was already there, and Mom said, "I'll make us some spaghetti. You go do some work. We'll talk after dinner."

Stephanie did all the talking during dinner, yapping away about a game of tag at recess where some kid got all scraped up when she tripped on the hard-top. About halfway through, Steph says, "What's wrong? Something's wrong."

"Nothing," I say real quick.

But Mom says, "Jake has an issue at school that is his own business, and he will share it with you at another time if he chooses to. For now, though, he would appreciate not having to explain it or talk about it. Do you understand?"

Under normal circumstances, that wouldn't be enough to put a cork in Steph, but something in Mom's voice must have told her to back off. So we ate the rest of dinner in silence.

"Stephanie and I will do the dishes," Mom said when we were finished. "You go ahead and get most of your work done and we'll talk around nine or so. Is that OK?"

It was, and at nine I came downstairs and found Mom at the desk in her study wearing her old pink terry-cloth bathrobe and the bunny slippers Stephie and I gave her for Christmas last year. She looked old. Her hair was back in a ponytail, which made the gray at her temples more obvious. The circles under her eyes were almost as dark as her eyebrows, making her look like an old, washed out third-base coach with eyeblack on. She usually wears something on her lips, but they looked chapped and dry tonight, and she looked even skinnier than usual in that big robe. I sort of realized that I don't usually look at her much in a careful, specific way, just in the general way you look at a parent. She looked weak and worn-down.

Our conversation went on until eleven. We talked about everything. In fact, I never talked to Mom quite like that before. It was almost like we were the same age just hanging out. We talked about Dad. She misses him still. Even after her marriage to my stepfather and their divorce, she still thinks about Dad. She still gets angry about him dying so young, and she feels lonely sometimes.

She worries about me at school, and I told her *I* was worried about me at school. I told her about how there was too much to do and how I was just keeping my head above water. But I also told her again that I liked the place even though I didn't think I did until this happened.

She seemed to understand that and said, "Being part of a community that cares enough about its members to hold them up to high expectations, to demand that they give the best of themselves, is really special."

I'd never thought about it exactly that way. I think she's mostly right, but I also like that everybody knows everybody else's name.

Nobody's set up higher than anybody else. You can even talk to the teachers, and they even want to talk to you. The seniors aren't just into themselves, and they know us by name, too. I said all that to her, and she seemed to agree.

We talked about Stephie and how she can be a pain in the neck. Mom said she just wants my attention, which she doesn't get much of anymore now that I'm so busy. We talked about my learning to drive, and we laughed about the way she gives directions, and I imitated her and she said, "I don't sound like that, Jake. You know I don't sound that bad!"

"Worse," I said. "Much worse," and she threw her glasses case at me, which I caught and threw back at her.

We didn't talk about the specifics of my stupidity. She said that she understood what had happened. She didn't excuse it, but she understood it. "The question," she said, "is where you go from here, what you learn from a mistake. That's the important thing."

We talked about that and how we both hoped they'd let me stay at St. Stephen's. But Mom said that we'd just have to live with whatever was decided and move along. When it got near eleven, she said, "Go on upstairs, honey, and get some sleep."

I said that I needed to do a little more work, and she kissed me and said goodnight.

Ms. White told me the next day I could stay. I have to get academic help. I have to speak to her and to some other people she wants me to see on Saturdays after community service. I need to write letters of apology to Ms. Marks and Mr. Meader, and I need to write an essay on what this whole thing means to me. I thought I was a goner for sure, so this was a huge relief. I felt like I'd won the lottery or something. Ms. White made it real clear that this kind of mistake was going to be my last. Another one will get me bounced because it will send a clear message that I either cannot learn from experience, or I do not care about honorable behavior. She was very stern, and her message was super clear. I could have kissed her! Mom was relieved. She tried to hold back her tears, but a few sneaked out.

On Friday, I met with the study skills teacher, and it wasn't the waste of time I had thought it would be. I should have gone earlier, like Mr. Meader suggested. I brought her my notebooks, and she looked them over. She said I don't have a clue about how to take notes or how to use them. "Don't write everything down. Listen carefully, and then write down what you think are central points. Summarize, in your own words, what's been said. Make big question marks where you might have missed something or where you don't understand."

She asked me if I had Physics homework and reading due tomorrow. I said, "Yeah," and she said, "Do it now." She watched me work for about half an hour. Then she stopped me. I'd just read the chapter and had started doing the problem assigned at the end. "All wrong," she said. "You need to approach your homework differently. First, *don't start with homework. Start with review.* Did you nail down the stuff from class today? Review your notes. Write down your questions. It'll take a little time now, but it will save you time later. Now, when you begin the assignment, don't just start reading. Read the assigned problems first. Ask yourself what you need to know to answer those questions. Then skim the chapter. Read the sub-headings. Look at the pictures and read the captions. Ask yourself what the chapter is about. Now start reading with a highlighter. *Highlight only those parts of the chapter that give you the information you need to answer the questions.* You are now working with purpose and direction, which will make you retain more and allow you to work more quickly."

It was all good stuff, and I didn't have a clue about any of it before. She's going to give me tips for Humanities and all my other courses. I think it'll make a big difference.

I'm sitting here on a Sunday night pretty much completely worn out. It really has been the week from hell. I was embarrassed when I talked to Mr. Meader and then to Ms. Marks, but they seemed to forgive me. They thanked me for my letters of apology and said "what's past is passed." I hope so. I don't want another week like this one. There's more to write about this past week, but more would probably be too much.

Chapter 8

Baltimore Sun Headlines, October 8-14

U.S. Lashes Back

Missiles, Bombs Pound Targets in Afghanistan

U.S. Claims Control of Skies

Anthrax Found in Third Worker at Paper in Florida

Fears Spread Over Anthrax

Bush Assails 'Evil One'

More Anthrax Cases Found

OCTOBER 9, 2001—SENIOR CHAPEL TALK,
DELIVERED BY WILLIAM JONES

It's my turn to honor the St. Stephen's Episcopal School tradition of the senior chapel talks. We are told to speak about something we care about deeply, that would be interesting to our fellow students, and that requires of us some degree of scholarship. So . . . as I look out from this pulpit at all of you sitting where I have been sitting for the past four years, I wonder, "What do you expect of me? What do you think I will talk about?" In fact, I want each of you to take a guess. I'll give you a few seconds to make a silent guess. OK. Let me guess first. Some of you know that I'm a nut for model airplanes. I build them and then fly them around on our back fields, or I used to fly them around until I steered my newest experiment through a closed, leaded window and into the Refectory. That was a memorable but final flight. Ms. White was not amused. Perhaps as many as two or three of you thought that would by my subject. If you did, please be honest and raise your hand. Ah, I miscalculated. Nobody picked that. Well, how about the short wave radio society I tried to start up? I made announcements for a solid month, every day all September, and nobody joined. Pity . . . How many of you chose that? Two hands! Excellent. It would have been a good speech. But, alas, no!

I know what you all think I'm going to talk about, and I hope you'll have the courage to admit it! Just about everyone in this old chapel thinks I'm going to talk about a subject related to race. Go ahead, raise your hands. I think fully eighty percent of you, faculty and students, have your hands in the air. Thanks for being honest, because this speech would be in some deep you-know-what if you'd decided not to cooperate.

Race! What else would a black student like me talk about in America? Your expectations, and the fact that I am about to fulfill those expectations, is a central illustration of what I intend to say to you this morning.

Before I get into my talk, I need to set a few things straight in case you misunderstand exactly where I'm coming from.

I do believe that America's "peculiar institution" was an atrocity that has few parallels in world history. And it didn't end with the Emancipation Proclamation that freed slaves only in the Confederate States. It didn't end with the Fifteenth Amendment. It didn't end in 1954 with *Brown v. Board of Education*, and it didn't end with the Civil Rights Acts and Voting Rights Act of 1964 and 1965 respectively. The centuries-old, crippling, and degrading reach of slavery is alive even now. Our society continues to pay a heavy price for the great compromise that allowed us to draft a constitution acceptable to both sections of the country—North and South—a compromise that allowed so-called men of idealism like Washington, Adams, Jefferson, Madison, and Monroe to sign their names to a document declaring some people only three-fifths human.

I further believe that racism, both overt and subtle, is alive and well in our country. I believe that otherwise foolish measures such as busing school children were unfortunate necessities. I believe that affirmative action has indeed accomplished much of what it set out to accomplish, giving us the likes of Colin Powell, Condoleeza Rice, Cornell West, Clarence Thomas, and others too many to mention, who never would have had a chance without that initial boost.

I believe all these things, and I hope you will not forget that in light of my central point.

To paraphrase a man whom we have all read in religion class, Martin Buber, "Before a man is of one race or another, he is first of all, and most importantly, a human being." Yet, a new myth has arisen, and it conspires to rob me of my humanity: "All African Americans think the same way, and if they don't, they're not authentic."

I'll turn eighteen in January, and I intend to register as a Republican. Surprised?

My father is a graduate of Harvard and a partner in the largest law firm in Baltimore City. My mother went to Spellman in Atlanta, and then to the Johns Hopkins Medical School. She's an OB-GYN at Union Memorial Hospital. I am not here on financial aid. Surprised?

I like some rap music, but much of it disgusts me. I don't wear my pants around my knees, and I'm a lousy dancer. Surprised?

When it comes to athletics, I may be the single most uncoordinated member of the senior class. Surprised?

Many of you are, and of those who aren't surprised, many of you are thinking, "Well, he's a sell-out. He's an 'Uncle Tom.' He's not really black, not authentic, lost touch with his roots." The saddest part of all is that much of that kind of silly thinking comes from the black community itself. When I use words that educated people routinely use, I'm asked, "Why you talk so white? Why you puttin' on airs and talkin' so white?" Congressman J.C. Watts from Oklahoma is called an "Uncle Tom" because he's a Republican. Justice Clarence Thomas is called a traitor because he's a conservative jurist. The message is clear: "Talk like us, think like us, act like us, or you ain't one of us, home boy!" The melanin in my skin is supposed to control my mind, my spirit, and my heart to one acceptable perspective. I'm expected to be more of a black man than I am a human.

And many white people, even well-intended white people, often do the same thing. I believe that my grades and my scores warrant acceptance at Stanford, to which I have applied early. If that acceptance occurs, there will be the knowing look. "Ah, yes, he's in the special category. He didn't really earn it." They'll ignore the fact that my SAT's are 1520, my grades place me near the top of the class, and I have more Advanced Placement Scores above 4 than anyone else in school. If I get into Stanford, they'll say, "His skin got him in."

There's an assumption that I'm from the 'hood, wherever that is, that I'm disadvantaged, that I'm a liberal, that I like certain food, music, and clothing, and that I'm a great athlete—all the stereotypes are alive and well in the white community. When they admit me into school, or give me a job, or ask me over to dinner, there's an assumption that I'll eat with my feet or won't recognize a fork. White people feel good that they're helping a poor little black boy get ahead.

This stuff makes me really angry, and I hope I've made my point. I am a human being first and a black man second. My race should not define me. Yet in a strange, ironic turn-about, our "peculiar institution" has reached across the years and affected my life in ways that are perversely funny.

So here I am, the privileged child of talented and dedicated parents who benefited from affirmative action's boost. Blacks see me as not black and not authentic, and whites assume my inferiority and my mindset. What's the answer?

For us in the black community, we need to stop defining ourselves by the criminal element. Those strutting punks whose lyrics celebrate rape and murder and who get their looks and their 'tude straight from the pen are not black culture. Langston Hughes is black culture. Duke Ellington is black culture. Wynton Marsalis is black culture. Ben Carson is black culture. Oprah Winfrey, one of the most powerful people in the world, is black culture. We need to start by admiring them, not Snoop Doggy Dogg, or Ray Lewis, or O.J. Simpson. We need to recognize that education is good, that there are as many ways in this country for a black man to succeed as there are for a white man.

Second, all of us need to get rid of laws that promote relying on government. Perhaps it is time for affirmative action to end. I don't know that for sure, but I know it shouldn't be permanent. The only way African-Americans will ever be seen as Americans, as humans first and as African-Americans second, will be when enough of us attain economic power to influence society. And that's up to us. Other marginalized groups who have suffered terrible atrocities have managed to gain power and respect in this country. The Jews are an example. Their strong emphasis on families and education, even in the face of centuries of discrimination and the Holocaust, should give us hope. Yes, that situation is different, but it should offer us hope.

Finally, to all of my white classmates, fellow students, and faculty members, don't assume *anything* about the next black man you meet. Just as you assume nothing about the next white person you meet, assume nothing about me. I may be a conservative. I may be a liberal. I may be poor. I may be rich. Whatever I am, I am first and foremost a human being, with all the strengths and all the weaknesses, all the problems, and all the joys, of every other human being.

Thank you.

JOURNAL ENTRY: OCTOBER 13, 2001

It was embarrassing, being back at school this week. I sort of assumed everyone was looking at me funny. But it was just in my head, I guess. I thought it'd be hard to talk to Mr. Meader and Ms. Marks, but they were cool. Ms. Marks told me that the past was passed, and we were going to move forward. She did give me a zero on that paper, and it'll be hell to raise my grade up. By the end of the week, I felt like things were back to normal. Lots of work and not enough sleep.

I can tell already that the study skills stuff works. She's helping me with my writing, too. I should have gone when Mr. Meader told me to go because I'm going to be able to cut major time off some of my homework assignments. I've been spinning my wheels on stuff that doesn't deserve much attention. The tricks of figuring out what's important and then remembering it—it just works.

Mr. Meader says I can cut back a little on the journal volume. I still need to write stuff every week, but I don't have to do more than I can handle. When I get my academics more under control, he says he'll turn the heat up again.

Our soccer team is awesome. We've only lost three games—all by one goal—and they have me at halfback on the right side. I don't mind the running, and I seem to be able to see the field pretty well. Our varsity soccer team is having a tough year, and that sucks, but they graduated a bunch of seniors last year who took the team all the way to the championship game, where they lost to a team they split with during the season.

This Saturday was a little crazy. Joel and me and three other guys were cleaning up Stoney Run, where the creek curves under University Parkway near Johns Hopkins. The bridge down there has some of the most amazing graffiti you've ever seen. It smells like piss, though, and I think a bunch of homeless guys sleep under there. We found a bunch of syringes and stuff, which Joel told us not to touch. He picked them up with his work gloves real carefully, and told us that these things were deadly from HIV and hepatitis contamination.

Then, I went around the edge of the creek, out from under the bridge, and saw what I thought was a brownish-green burlap sack for corn or grain or something. It was half in the water and half out. When I got close, and I could see it was a greasy old army jacket on a person, I just about pissed my pants. He was face down in the water, where it's about two and a half feet deep. His legs, which were in these ripped and grubby old pants, were sticking stiff and straight into the grass on the bank. I fell down twice trying to get away from that body, and I started screaming for Joel. He came running over, and I showed him the body. He was pale when he turned toward me, but he was real calm. "Go up on University Parkway. Go into a building and ask if you can use the phone for a 911 call. They'll let you if you say it's a police matter. Take one of those guys with you—take Jordie—and then wait for the police to come. I'll stay here with the other guys and with the body."

I did what he said and a cop showed up with his siren on about two minutes after I called. I took him down the steep bank to Stoney Run, where the body was. Everything after that is a blur. A bunch of police came down. And somehow an ambulance managed to find a way through the woods and across a field to about fifty yards from the body. They asked us all kinds of questions, and to keep people away from the scene, they set up a crime scene area with yellow tape attached to trees and stakes. A crowd gathered, and everyone was curious.

It seemed to me that some old bum or some druggy might have gone to sleep near the water and just rolled in. Did he get mugged? He didn't look like the kind of guy who would have anything anybody would want.

We didn't get any cleaning up done because they didn't finish with us until our community service time was up. We jammed into Joel's nasty old Ford Taurus, which we took today instead of a school van because Mr. Meader couldn't make it, and we drove back to school.

On the drive, Jordie, a real talkative ninth grader, piped up from way in the back. "A dead homeless bum isn't much of a loss." I thought Joel was going to drive off the road. He sort of twisted around to get a look at Jordie, and said, "That's a pretty shitty thing to say."

"Why?" Jordie said. "He's probably an alcoholic or a drug addict, and he probably steals stuff. And you know darn well he doesn't do anything for anybody else."

"I don't know any of those things," Joel said, "and neither do you."

"But I bet I'm right. And if I am right, who cares about that guy? He's better off dead."

"You should care, that's who."

"Why should I care?"

"Because he's a human being."

"Yeah, right, he's a real prize, the kind of guy you want marrying your sister," said Jordie, who got a good laugh from everybody but Joel.

Joel's tone of voice changed after a few seconds of silence, after the laughter stopped. "Would it make any difference to you if the man was a war hero?" asked Joel. "What if he's a family man with schizo-phrenia, who's regular when he's taking his medication, but loses con-trol when he's not? What if he's mentally handicapped and can't take care of himself? What then, Jordie?"

"When they're just a drag on society, they're no big loss when they're dead."

"So we should euthanize crippled people and old people? So we should cull out the weak?"

"I didn't say that."

"It sounded pretty close to me. How do you judge a society, any-way? By the way it treats its wealthy and successful people? Every soci-ety treats them well. Or do you measure a society by the way it cares for those who cannot care for themselves? What kind of place, Jordie, do you want our country to be?"

Well, that conversation continued all the way back to school. That's a first in my lifetime—being around a bunch of kids who discuss a big issue without any teacher or parent or coach around to make them do it, at least since my stepbrother Hank moved away, because he seemed to think about everything. Jordie wouldn't back down at all even though Joel is way smart. Jordie said that poor people are always around in every society and always will be, that it was twisting his words to say he was in favor of euthanasia. His point was that a soci-ety has little to cry about when an individual who is a mere parasite dies. Joel and Jordie were like mini-adults, going back and forth, each with good points. It felt good to be part of that, like we were doing something real.

When we got back to school, I had to stay to meet with some guy named Judge Walker. Ms. White was in her office when I knocked on the door. She was talking to the same old white-haired man who had walked into the chapel with her on the first day of school.

"Jake, I'd like you to meet retired Court of Appeals Justice Horace Walker, who is the chairman of our Board of Trustees. Judge Walker, this is Jake Phillips, a new tenth grader at St. Stephen's."

We shook hands and sat down. Ms. White said she would leave us together for a few hours, that I should tell Judge Walker what my situation was, and that Judge Walker would take over from there. She left, and the Judge asked me to go ahead. So I told him about the plagiarism. He asked me a bunch of questions about it, and I told him the same things I'd told everyone else. Then he handed me a book with a marker in it, and told me to open it up. He said I should read aloud to him, and he would stop me every so often to ask me some questions.

The story is called "Crito" and was written by Plato about a conversation between Socrates and Crito while Socrates is in jail. It sounded like the whole thing would be pretty boring, but it turned out not to be. Judge Walker was pretty cool too. He sure did love this Crito. The main gist of the conversation seems to be that Socrates won't escape from jail even though Crito can spring him and even though Socrates is innocent. He's going to die instead, a decision I still don't really buy into completely. But Socrates is so dedicated to a concept—living truthfully and honorably and consistent with an ideal—that he would rather be dead than be alive and a hypocrite. We skipped over some stuff, but we read most of it and talked about lots of it. He interrupted me a lot to talk about things. The two hours went by fast. He's kind of a neat old dude.

The other thing about this week has been the anthrax stuff. People are starting to freak out that it's gonna take over the world and that we're all going to die from diseases that the terrorists are going to spread. It just doesn't seem likely to me.

Chapter 9

Baltimore Sun Headlines, October 15-21

Anthrax Spores Found on 3 More

Big Anthrax Attack Could Overwhelm System, Experts Fear

No Link Yet to Anthrax, bin Laden

Similarities Detected in Letter Sent to Daschle and Brokaw

Anthrax Alert Shuts House of Representatives

'Substantive Leads' Found

Anxious Americans Flock to Mexico for Cheap Cipro

Anthrax Reward: $1 Million

On Guard Against Bioterrorism

Postal Route in NJ Tracked

OCTOBER 18, 2001—CHAPEL TALK,
DELIVERED BY RECTOR MARY WHITE

Because of September 11th, and now with bioterrorism promi-
nently featured in the news, our sense of security in this country is fragile. Certainly not since the nuclear attack drills that we conducted in the 1950s and '60s have schools had to take so seriously the
possibility that we are under a real threat. It is very hard to see that
much good can come out of such tragedy and such fear. Too many
people have lost loved ones. More attacks remain possible. None of

that is good.

If, however, we are to go forward from the horror of recent events, we must not wallow in our fears and our sorrows. Hope is far from lost, and I think it is even possible to renew ourselves through the challenges of our insecurity.

These recent events have forced us to recognize the impermanence and fragility of our lives. As we watch the brave firemen dig through the Trade Center rubble, as we see the pictures and missing persons posters collecting on the wall in New York City, we cannot help considering the suddenness of this catastrophe. Thousands of healthy people engaged in their daily routine were snuffed out in an instant. Few could say good-bye. Few could reach their loved ones. One second—alive. The next—dead.

We have been confronted with our own mortality. The precarious nature of the human condition has been unavoidably thrust in our faces. "In the end, we are all dead," or as Hobbes put it, "Life is nasty, brutish, and short." This elemental truth binds us all together in a shared situation. We all know, if anybody asks us, that we don't have much time on this earth, yet few of us live as though time is precious and life could end in the next moment. When we are young, the whole idea of death seems unreal. It doesn't seem possible that it will happen to us. We are young, and healthy, and vibrant, and so very alive, that death is a long way off in a distant land. Yet, none of us can know that with anything close to certainty.

The truth of our mortality genuinely internalized and understood can do nothing other than increase our empathy for our fellow human beings. If we let it, it brings to us the grace of humility. "From dust we came, and to dust we shall return." This humble empathy can be the starting point for serious reflection, for genuine kindness, for commitment to make meaningful all the moments of your life. Mere accumulation of creature comforts seems less important. Relationships and community seem more important.

But very few of us manage to learn this lesson early in our lives. I wonder if even the tragedies we are living today are getting our attention. I'm not sure that the old gray head you see peeking out at you from behind this lectern would have learned the lessons of humility inherent in our fragile mortality when she was your age. In fact, I learned no such thing. And I worry that each of us must come to that understanding the hard way, through personal experience.

For me, it was a combination of events in quick succession when I was twenty-five years old. I had met my husband, a dashing fourth-year midshipman, elegant in his crisp white uniform, while I was an undergraduate at Goucher College. I went to a dance at the Naval Academy in the autumn, and he simply stole my heart. He was graduated in May and received a Marine Corps commission. In June, we were married in that sublime Naval Academy Chapel. For three years, I accompanied him from base to base. My favorite was San Diego. My least favorite, Parris Island.

But we had each other, and we cared about little else. I could find work as a teacher wherever we went, and I had him. Then he got his orders for Southeast Asia. He was a young captain, on the fast track, a tremendous success. Fourteen months after he left for Vietnam, I got a visit I'll never forget. A chaplain, a Marine Corps colonel, and a driver pulled up in a black sedan in front of my parents' house in Homewood, right here in Baltimore, where I had come to live while Davey was overseas. They told me he had been killed—the helicopter he was in was shot down. The impact killed four of them. He was gone.

Vanished in an instant were all my comfortable assumptions about how life would be. It was 1965, and I was twenty-five years old, and I simply couldn't believe that this could happen. I knew people were killed in war, but not my Davey. Surely it was not possible.

Only a month later, still almost paralyzed from grief, I discovered a lump in by breast. I ignored it. I denied that it was possible. But three months later, pretending everything was fine became impossible, and a visit to the doctor confirmed what I would not allow myself to believe. I had breast cancer. A radical mastectomy followed. I was only twenty-five.

This was the physical, emotional, and spiritual crisis of my life. I was unprepared for the fragility of my own life, the mortality of my husband, and my own mortality. Up to this point, I had made the blithe and unexamined assumption that in my life, everyone I cared about, including me, would live happily ever after. Because of a benign sort of unspoken arrogance, I didn't have to mind the reality of our shared human condition. I had not lived my life to that point with a genuine respect for life's preciousness. I was cavalier about the wealth of life and time that seemed to crash over me undeserved and unearned.

It was through the love and nurturing of others that I managed to piece myself together. I landed a job at this wonderful school at age twenty-seven and found in it a source of purpose and meaning that had eluded me before. Before my tragedies, I hadn't been looking for purpose and meaning. Now, chastened by the unavoidable truth that all humans share, I approached each day with humble thanks that I had another day to enjoy. I made a conscious effort, sometimes successful, sometimes less so, to make the best of every moment. I became much more open to what life and other people's lives had to offer me, and what small gifts I could offer in return.

It is such a shame, such a pity, that it took biting personal tragedy to get my attention. Like a mule, I had to be hit between the eyes before I could really focus on what mattered. Perhaps, in your lives, this may be the great gift of September 11th. Perhaps this national tragedy will teach you the humbling lesson that life is short and time is precious. If so, a whole world opens to you. Your education will take on added meaning. You will be grateful for your classmates and your teachers, and for the opportunities in your lives. You will take advantage of things you might have taken for granted. September 11th may be able to teach you in a way that other events cannot—that truth and beauty and kindness and love are what give your life meaning. If we can learn that lesson from these horrible tragedies, then indeed, we have been able to fashion some good out of bad. That is my hope for you today.

JOURNAL ENTRY: OCTOBER 21, 2001

Anthrax is on everybody's brain. They brought in a biology and communicable disease professor from the University of Maryland to talk to us in chapel about this whole biological terrorism thing. It turns out that anthrax is pretty tough to catch. You can't get it from another person; in other words, it's not contagious. That's a relief.

You can get it on your skin, in which case you get a real bad zit that turns into a nasty sore. That's called cutaneous. The inhaled kind looks just like the flu, and since it's rare, that's what most people mistake it for. By the time you figure out you have anthrax and not the flu, you're probably dead meat. If you do diagnose early anthrax, it's real easy to treat with antibiotics. Everyone's talking about running to the pharmacy and getting a ton of Cipro, which is the best stuff for killing anthrax. This expert says that's a waste of money. He says that the "widespread dissemination of anthrax requires too much sophistication for it to be a viable terrorist option." That's the way the guy spoke. You practically needed a translator. I admit, though, that I was a little scared like everyone else until this guy came in on Friday.

He was a little more worried about smallpox. An infected person doesn't become contagious until he's feeling really bad, but then he's real contagious. One sick guy staggering around the streets of a city could infect thousands of other people. Since the terrorists don't mind sacrificing their own lives, they could get themselves infected in another country, fly into the United States, let the germ incubate, get really sick, and then infect as many people as possible before croaking. He could go to a stadium, or a train station, or an airport. That's pretty scary stuff. It sounds as though our country ought to start stocking up on the vaccine again.

Ms. White spoke to us early in the week about how we ought to make September 11th and all this terrorism stuff into a positive by understanding we're all going to die. Pretty depressing if you ask me. Boy, has she gone through some nasty experiences. Her husband was killed in Vietnam, and I didn't even know she was married. Then she got breast cancer, which nearly killed her. Somehow she pulled through the whole thing and became a teacher here at St. Stephen's. She must be a pretty tough lady, but that's not how she comes across at all. It's sort of like we're all her children. She treats us like that. I've gotten to know her from our conversations after my big screw-up, and she's pretty cool. You'd never know, just from how she is around school, that she'd been through that kind of horrible sadness and sickness. I would think having your breasts chopped off when you're a young woman would be a major downer.

This week has been the usual hard work, but I'm feeling more confident that I can handle it. Physics and Geometry I'm good at. I'm not like one of the top guys or anything, but I'm pretty solid. It's Humanities and French that are just about killing me. You'd think they'd let us ask a question in English when we don't get something in French class, but no, it's got to be in French. Even extra help is in French.

In Humanities, if you write a paper, which we do just about every minute of every day, it seems, you get it back covered in red pencil corrections the next day. You are expected to make the corrections and take the teacher's suggestions and turn the paper back in again. When you've done that, you are likely to get it back again with more red pencil marks and more suggestions, and you have to resubmit it again. Once you and the teacher are satisfied with the paper, it goes into a portfolio to be evaluated by the Humanities Department to determine your term grade. The process takes forever, and while you're doing it, you still get new assignments and daily reading.

About once a week, we get a long lecture in the lecture hall from someone in the Art Department or the Music Department that coincides with the period of history we're learning about. We take notes, and they're submitted for review by the teacher. I'm taking better notes now with the advice the study skills person gave me.

The Saturday clean-up was pretty cool this week. There were a bunch of us, so Mr. Meader drove us out in a school van. Some guy must have backed his truck into the overgrown lot of a torn-down old factory on Falls Road and dumped a pile of crap right along the bank and into the Jones Falls. There were about twenty tires, dozens of big drums of stuff, and all kinds of garbage that looked like it came out of a garage or a mechanics shop or something—rusted out steel benches, busted-up tools, big oily canvas sheets, and a steel sink with a hole in it.

We made a big pile of the stuff in the middle of the lot. The kitchen had made us a bunch of sandwiches and given us a case of Cokes, so we sat there eating and talking. It was a nice day, almost hot, and the sun was out and bright. There were two great blue herons that we didn't seem to scare much. Usually you get within fifty yards, and they croak their crackly croak and fly off, but these guys, one downstream and one upstream, didn't seem to mind us, even though they were maybe as close as thirty yards or so.

While we were eating lunch, we started talking about those dorky birds. Mr. Meader said that these two are pretty brave compared to most, and they almost always steer clear of people. He told us about one that managed to step into some sort of steel trap and couldn't get its legs out. It was just stuck near the bank when some guy saw it. He watched it for awhile and then went over to try to free it. When he got close, the bird went just about nuts trying to get away. It flopped around and flapped its wings. The guy tried to grab it, but the bird was swinging its big old pointy beak around so hard it was like a dagger. The guy took a shot to the shoulder and it gashed him really bad and broke his collar bone, so he backed off. Every time he started toward it again, it started to struggle. The stupid bird was going to die if it didn't get help, but it was fighting off the one thing that could save it. It was just too terrified, too wild, too suspicious to let anybody helpful get close.

Finally, the guy quit and went to get help. He didn't come back because he had to go to the hospital, but four of his friends stepped in. They threw a blanket over the bird and got it under control. Then, working as a team, they managed to hold it down while they freed its legs. One leg was almost broken off. Instead of letting the bird go, they managed to get it to some place that rehabs injured wild animals. Last Mr. Meader heard, they were getting ready to return the heron to the wild.

That bird was unlucky and lucky at the same time. Who would expect there to be a big old trap right where you're walking? There you are, doing your heron thing, and, "Wham!" you're stuck in a trap through no fault of your own. Like what part in your evolution could prepare you for a trap? He nearly kills someone trying to help him and the guy doesn't give up. He might've just told the heron to cram it and left it to die. Instead, it got more than it deserved when a group came by and saved its sorry ass. Then they took it to a place where there must have been animal docs to fix it, and then folks to feed it and nurse it back to health. That's a bunch of good luck for one unlucky bird, and my guess is that it was too dumb to be grateful.

A pickup truck came by, and we threw all the crap into the back. The driver was one of the maintenance guys from school. I don't know where he was going to take all that garbage. Then we loaded back into the van and headed for St. Stephen's. I had to spend a couple hours that afternoon with the Judge. I read *Antigone*, a play by a Greek named Sophocles, out loud to the Judge, and he asked me questions every once in awhile. It's a pretty good story. King Creon says that if any of his citizens tries to bury one of his dead enemies, the citizen won't get buried either, which was a pretty big deal. His own nephew fights against him and is killed, so Creon says he can't get buried. Then Antigone, who is Creon's niece, tells Creon to shove it, and she buries her brother, Creon's enemy, who she loves. Creon gets pissed and locks up Antigone in a cave. When he finally decides to let her go, he finds out she's killed herself. Creon seems like something of a prick, but it's hard to see why his nephew shouldn't have to obey the laws like everyone else.

Antigone is a heavy thinker. She decided to break the law, and she understands exactly what's going to happen if she does. She's willing to take whatever comes her way. The King seems more emotional, like he's always doing stuff because he's pissed off, not because he's figured out what the right thing is. Even though he's technically right, he's wrong. Even though Antigone broke the law, she's right. Funny how she didn't seem to mind the law as much until it hurt her. I guess that's pretty typical of everybody. But, Antigone had thought things through pretty well. Too bad she couldn't have stood the cave for a little longer because it would have ended right if she'd been a little tougher. Maybe she was claustrophobic or something.

Mom picked me up, and I drove us home. I'm getting pretty confident behind the wheel. I think I'm ready for the road driving test now, but I've got to put in more hours driving before I can convert my learner's permit into an actual license.

Today, Sunday, was the usual: church, homework, a little fishing on the Gunpowder, where I caught a lunker of a brown deep in a pool, and then homework, and then more homework, and then more homework . . .

Chapter 10

Baltimore Sun Headlines, October 22-28
House, Senate Office Buildings to Stay Closed
2 Mailworkers Die, 2 Ill, Anthrax is Suspected
4 New Cases of Anthrax in Maryland, New Jersey
'No Guarantees' That Mail is Safe, Postmaster Says
Probe Has Found No Links Between Anthrax, September 11
Officials Widen Hunt for Anthrax

OCTOBER 23, 2001—SENIOR CHAPEL TALK,
DELIVERED BY BERNIE PANCIERA

At St. Stephen's, we pride ourselves in our openness to ideas. We get a liberal education in the humanities, mathematics, and the sciences, and we believe that reasoned discussion, even open, rational disagreement and argument are important. Many of our teachers use the Socratic method, constantly questioning us and forcing us to reach our own conclusions. But one question in our country has infected even this school. It is hard to discuss rationally. People have invested too much of themselves. They feel too strongly. Often they dismiss those who disagree with them in hateful terms or with patronizing condescension reserved for the stupid.

I am talking about abortion. I have been raised a Roman Catholic, and my parents are pro-life. My older sister, Sheila, is a senior at the University of Virginia, a Planned Parenthood supporter, and an active pro-choicer. Last July we had a dinner conversation that ended with shouting. Sheila left the table, left the house, and didn't come home for a week. That can happen if your own parents call you a murderer. In their defense, however, Sheila had treated them like complete dummies, called them religious reactionaries, and suggested they were brainwashed zombies of the Pope.

That's when I decided to look into this issue. I started to read up on it during August, and then, when I got to school in September, I started to approach various teachers. I was disappointed to discover that even here at St. Stephen's, people get emotional and crazy very easily on the abortion subject. I turned the tables on my teachers by using the Socratic method on them. Since I know the subject pretty well from my reading, it wasn't hard to get folks to a point where they resorted to clichés or anger. One group doesn't seem any more or less reasonable than the other.

In the context of September 11th, it is particularly upsetting to see evidence of what I could call the "Taliban mentality" right here at home. That is, "If you disagree with me, you are either stupid or evil, and there can be no other explanation." One person said to me, "To say a zygote is a human being is just stupid." Another said, "Pro-choicers advocate murder, and abortionists are murderers. Period. End of story." Those are exact quotes from teachers in this school. I am disappointed.

I have become a reluctant and hesitant quasi-pro-choicer who could be persuaded differently if a new and original argument tipped the balance toward pro-life. Here's the trail I took to my current position.

Jake

I went to the landmark decision *Roe v. Wade* and read the whole opinion. Justice Harry Blackmun struggled mightily to shape a common sense, science-based approach to the issue. He divided pregnancy into trimesters. He considered the status of the unborn. He considered the rights of women to control their own bodies, their own reproductive functions. There is little that Blackmun didn't consider. It's a really interesting opinion, and most people who have strong feelings about it have not read it.

Roe v. Wade made abortion a constitutional right. There's no mention of abortion, of course, in the U.S. Constitution, so strict constructionists, those who believe the Constitution should be applied, not interpreted, feel that the Supreme Court overstepped its bounds. Even some, who agree with the result the Supreme Court reached, feel that in fashioning a compromise, Blackmun and the court acted too much like a legislature. The court found that in "the penumbra"—and nobody really knows what that means—of the Constitution, you can find a right of privacy. The court then decided in a case called *Griswold v. Connecticut* that within that right of privacy there was a right to reproductive control that could not be infringed by a state. *Roe v. Wade*'s abortion right was a logical next step, according to some who agree with the decision.

Whether the Supreme Court or a state legislature or our national Congress should be making the abortion decision is a complicated side issue that can get in the way of thinking about abortion itself. So I started over, from the beginning.

What is abortion? I have defined it as ending a pregnancy on purpose before it has run its natural, biological course. I have defined pregnancy as a fertilized egg in a woman's uterus, and I'm going to ignore the knotty issue of whether a pregnancy includes a fertilized egg in a petrie dish.

The next question is the crux of the matter because any society calling itself civilized recognizes the sanctity of innocent human life. Our Declaration of Independence embodies this as "self-evident," that "we are endowed by our creator with certain inalienable rights" and that one of these rights is "life." This is John Locke's Enlightenment idea of natural rights. So, my premise is that every society has a legitimate interest in protecting innocent human life. The question then is, "What is a human life?" or, "What is it to be a human?" or, "When does human life begin?"

I'm here to tell you that I am no more confident of my conclusion now than I was when I began to answer the question. I'm not going to try to walk you through all the twists and turns this problem presents. To those who assert confidently that a zygote is not a human being, let me suggest that your confidence is misplaced. Why isn't it a human? Because it doesn't look human? Well, many badly burned or horribly deformed people don't look human. Because it is undeveloped? Well, retarded people are undeveloped. Because it has no consciousness? Well, people in a coma have no consciousness. Because it is completely dependent on a mother and cannot exist without her? Well, that defines a newborn baby or people who are quadriplegics. Once you get on the slippery slope of trying to decide when life starts after conception and to draw a developmental distinction or a technological distinction or a scientific distinction, you are in logical trouble. Your argument won't survive scrutiny.

So, I don't know when a human life starts, but I am certainly open to the idea that it starts at conception. Perhaps then, if you've accepted my premise that civilized society protects innocent human life, you are asking, "How could this guy be pro-choice?"

I cannot dismiss the idea that a woman has the right to control her own body, to control her own biological process. This seems to be the most private of matters—affairs of the womb. Do we want the government of the United States, a state government, or any other external agency reaching into a womb and regulating its workings? That makes me uncomfortable. It is the ultimate Big Brother at work. It is the definition of invasive. It is the blatant violation of privacy.

Since I believe that reasonable people can draw reasoned and thoughtful decisions on opposite sides of defining what a human is or when life begins, that leads me to then ask who should be making such a decision. Do we want a government doing it? Do we want a matter of opinion enforced uniformly on all people regardless of their beliefs? If people knew, really knew, when human life began, and if it were not an issue upon which reasonable people could disagree, this question would be an easier one for me. But regardless of the vehement assertions of truth, nobody knows with certainty.

So I leave this decision in the beginning to the mother. I do it reluctantly, but I do it. She has an interest that is undeniable. The government's interest in protecting innocent human life is also undeniable, but in this case it is qualified only because neither the government nor anyone else knows when life begins.

But I do believe that the government does have an interest. History since *Roe v. Wade* shows that abortion has become a casual, routine undertaking. It's almost a method of birth control. In truth, though, it is a huge decision, a moral decision. The government has an interest in making sure that innocent human life is protected. The government should regulate abortions.

First, minors should absolutely not be able to get abortions without consulting their parents. They are not ready to handle such a responsibility without careful, thoughtful adult input. If people at a certain age are not old enough to drink, or to drive, or to vote, they certainly are not ready to deal with all the implications of the abortion decision.

Second, the government should not subsidize abortions in any way. The government must be neutral. While it should not ban some personal decisions, it also should not encourage them. Does this make abortions less available to the poor? Perhaps. But the government cannot be asked to cure every problem that arises because of limited resources, and the interest of protecting innocent life is more important than preserving options.

Third, the government should support, promote, encourage and subsidize pre-natal care, help with post-natal expenses, adoption, and any other service that promotes the healthy and safe delivery and upbringing of children. All pre-conception birth control should be free. People who adopt children should receive tax credits.

Fourth—this is really controversial and exactly what Justice Blackmun tried to do—the government should be allowed to draw an arbitrary line in the sand. They should be able to say that, "We don't know exactly when a zygote becomes a fetus, and a fetus becomes a human being, but we know it does happen. When it does happen, we intend to assert our interest in preserving human life." I would suggest the end of the first trimester as that common sense point. Birth is too late. Conception is too early. That's my opinion, nothing more. I understand its strengths and its weaknesses. It merely recognizes that at some point before birth, an innocent human life begins.

In conclusion, let me say only that we should not think like the Taliban, not at this school, not anywhere. Decent people can disagree. We need to listen carefully and completely and hold our opinions in humility. In exploring this issue, the only people I have disdain for are the zealots—those who would deny to others the integrity of their beliefs. Thank you.

Jake

I'm way past pissed off! She felt a goddamn lump in August. You don't need to be a fucking brain surgeon to know you ought to go to a doctor. Shit, the stupid breast cancer commercials on television are so obvious that even I know that, and I've never paid any attention. "Well, honey, the timing was bad." What kind of an excuse is that?! So she doesn't do shit until last week after she's found another lump in her armpit, and guess what? . . . DUH!! She's got herself not just breast cancer but a nice advanced case.

She tells me to think things through or live with the consequences. Well, it's not just her who has to live with these consequences. How about Stephie? How about me? I've been on the Internet. Advanced cases like the one she's describing have a piss-poor survival rate. She's got to have what they call a radical mastectomy. Even with all these new "less invasive" treatments, she's got to lose both her breasts. And there's stuff in her lymph nodes in her armpits and in her neck and she's got spots on her lungs. Didn't she think it was a little odd that Mrs. High-Energy was exhausted all the time?! After they cut that stuff out of her, she'll be doing chemotherapy and getting radiation. She'll be in the hospital for at least a week and then she'll be sick as a dog for a month. Then it's six goddamn more months of radiation and chemo when she'll feel awful. And then they'll "assess where they are." Even if the treatment goes well, which I understand from the net isn't all that likely, she won't know for six years whether it'll come back or not. Fuck her!

I don't even want to think about what happens next. No father. No cousins. Nothing but dead grandparents. Mom's brother died when she was little. If we have no mother, where is Stephie going to live? What am I going to do? This doesn't suck! It sucks and blows and bites!

Mom tells me all this on Wednesday. She gets operated on tomorrow, Monday. Stephie is staying with good friends from St. George's Church. I'm going to live at school for two weeks. I didn't even know about the dorm rooms up on the third floor of the main building. I went up and took a look. Four guys to a room with about five rooms. That's for sleeping. There's a study room with twenty carrels where we can keep all our books and stuff. Then there's a kitchen, large area with a CD player and a refrigerator and a bunch of comfortable chairs and couches. We eat all our meals in the refectory. There's a faculty apartment up there, too, and whoever lives there is the supervisor. I don't know who that is yet. That sucks! The whole fucking thing stinks.

I can't believe that just last week, Ms. White talked about her breast cancer. She called me into the office on Thursday morning to talk about Mom. I pretty much clammed up and said nothing. She said that Mom had a tough battle ahead of her, and she needed my help and support. She said that Mom didn't need to be worrying about anything but dealing with her illness. She hoped I would be a source of strength for Mom. She also said that it was natural to be afraid and that she would be surprised if I weren't scared. I didn't react to anything she said. I just sat there. Yeah, I'm scared, but I'm also pissed. I'm not ready to talk about this stuff.

Mr. Meader also took me into his office. We talked about the soccer team, and we talked about how my studies seem to be going well. I've gotten some good grades in Geometry and in Physics. We talked about the community service stuff I've been doing and the old guy we found in Stoney Run. Then we talked about the dormitory arrangement on the third floor. He told me how it worked, and said that he'd like to have me over for dinner at his house if I wanted. Mr. Meader's cool. He told me he was sorry to hear about Mom's cancer and said that if I needed to talk, he was available. He also said that he'd made an appointment for me with the school counselor. "You have no choice here, Jake. You're going to see Mrs. Conkling."

Whatever.

Chapter 11

Baltimore Sun Headlines, October 29-November 4

Anthrax Found in 5 More D.C. Buildings

2 Cases Challenge Beliefs on Who May Get Anthrax

Sweeping Probe Opens in N.Y. Anthrax Death

No Sign of More Resistant Anthrax

4 U.S. Soldiers Hurt in Afghan Chopper Crash

F.B.I. Asks for Help Tracking Anthrax

1,100 Buoy Kabul Forces

Md. Experts: Key Lessons on Anthrax Go Untapped

OCTOBER 31, 2001—HANDWRITTEN LETTER
TO JAKE FROM KAREN

Dearest Jake,

I wish you were not so angry with me, but I understand your feelings. And, of course, you're right. I've been foolish. I just couldn't bring myself to admit that I might be sick. It didn't seem possible, and I would not allow myself to consider the truth and its implications. Please forgive me. I cannot bear to have you so upset. And I do love you so. You and your sister are more precious to me than I can possibly express. I know that this may be hard for you to believe sometimes, given the demands I put on you. Now that my stupid refusal to seek medical help threatens my health and your security, it may be even harder for you to know the depths of my love. Have faith in it, though. Never doubt it. It is my deepest promise and gift to you.

I have faith. Faith that you will buck up and hang in there during my treatment. I have faith that God will somehow look after our little family. I have faith that He will give me strength to persevere in the face of this physical challenge. And Jake, I will persevere. Do not doubt for a moment that I will be back to my old self, being a pain in your neck, quicker than you think. It will not be easy, and I will need your help.

I'm writing you now only because I anticipate that a combination of drugs and discomfort will keep me under the weather for the next short while. I didn't want to miss this chance to let you know that I love you and believe in you. The way you reacted to your honor mistake made me very proud of you. You are becoming a fine young man, the kind of person your father and I hoped you would become. Good luck in the dormitory. Eat well. Get plenty of sleep. I'll see you soon.

Much love,
Mom

JOURNAL ENTRY: NOVEMBER 4, 2001

Stephie and I visited Mom in the hospital. She looked tiny in the white bed. She squeezed Stephie's hand so hard that Stephie yelped. She was teary and sort of groggy. Ms. White and Mr. Meader took us in. They stood quietly in the corner after wishing Mom well, and then they stood in the hallway while Mom and Stephie and me talked. It's impossible to stay angry with Mom for long, especially with her looking so helpless. She says the operation went well, better than expected. They're starting right in with the chemo and the radiation, and she claims things are looking good.

I wouldn't go that far. I've become kind of a breast cancer expert and have tried to pick through some of the crap people throw at you to try to make you feel good. From what I can tell, breast cancer usually starts out inside something called milk ducts that are spread out all through the breast. Some cells start to grow like crazy and the doctors don't have a clue why. Mom's tumor had gotten outside one of those ducts and was about 2.7 centimeters. Worse, it had somehow gotten involved with Mom's lymph nodes, which means the cancer travels to other places from there. The good news, if you can call it that, is that Mom has what they call fast-growing cancer. I'm not completely sure how they know this, but they claim that the cancer hasn't been in her that long and that it is an aggressive kind that responds well to treatment. I'm not sure I'm buying that explanation yet.

Mom's in what they call Stage III. That means she needs not just this mastectomy but also chemotherapy and radiation. They're also going to give her a drug called Tamoxifen for reasons that aren't completely clear to me. Things don't look quite as awful as they seemed at first. About half the people who go Stage III live for a minimum of five years.

The lymph nodes seem like the key to the whole deal. Both of Mom's breasts are a mess, and stuff in her armpits looks lousy too. But they turned out to be wrong about her lungs. They're clear. So if they cut all that crap out, radiate the hell out of her, and then flood her with chemo, she'll live. Maybe. But the treatment itself might make you wish you weren't alive. I guess it makes you feel sick and causes your hair to fall out, and it can actually burn you, too. She's in for some lousy times.

Life in the dorm is fine. Mr. Meader comes by every night to check on me like some kind of second mother. There's nothing to do really except eat, sleep, and study. The dorm master, Charlie Jackson, is the athletic trainer. He's a good guy. Every night at 10:00, he gets us ice cream or cookies or pizza or something to pig out on. There are ten of us in the dorm, so it's half empty. One of the guys has some sort of drug war going on in his neighborhood, so his mom doesn't want him at home. Another guy's parents are in the middle of a nasty divorce and were actually getting into physical fights with each other. He says his mother sneaked up behind his father while he was watching TV and smacked him on the head with a cast-iron frying pan, fractured his skull, and knocked him out cold, but he deserved it because he'd punched her in the eye. Nice stuff!

The school counselor, Mrs. Conkling, has met with me twice. It's not as ugly as I thought it was going to be. She didn't tell me a bunch of stuff, which was what I expected her to do. She just asked questions in a way that made it easy to answer, and then she would sit there in silence when you were finished so you felt like you needed to explain more. I'm betting that's some kind of technique they use to get kids to talk, but for some reason it didn't bother me.

Apparently it's pretty normal to get angry when your parent gets sick. In my case, it's not really anger. It's fear. I'd never really thought about all the stuff Mom does *for* me. It mostly seems like she does stuff *to* me. She is such a royal pain in the ass on so many levels that it's hard sometimes to get past the nagging and see that she's trying to be a good parent. I think she screws it up some by being too pissy about little stuff. My underwear on the floor does not seem like a big issue to me. Drinking out of the O.J. carton is not a felony in most people's houses. But on the big stuff, she's right there with you. The cheating stuff that nearly got me expelled was definitely major, but she didn't get nuts. She was quiet and reasonable the whole time. She wasn't happy—no question about that—but the whole thing seemed to depress and disappoint her more than make her angry.

A few years back, I snuck out of the house with Hank and went to a wild party. Things got out of hand, so I had to call her to rescue us. She was calm and cool about the whole thing, but there were major league consequences—lots of long talks but no yelling or dumb nagging. I also had to endure being guarded for a while. Mrs. Conkling has definitely helped me see my mother in a clearer way. Mom will be coming home sometime during this coming week. She wants me to keep on boarding during the first few days so she can get herself together. I don't like the idea, but I admit it's reasonable.

Yesterday our community service was pretty uneventful. All we did was pick up trash for a few hours, then head back to school. I spent two hours afterwards with the Judge. He gave me a present—a thick, heavy book called *The Book of Virtues*—and he said we didn't need to meet any more, that he was satisfied I understood the importance of honesty. We read from my new book, from a section called honesty. There's a conversation in there between Glaucon and Socrates from Plato's *Republic*. The main point, I think, is that honesty or justice or integrity or any virtue doesn't necessarily get you anything or anywhere in an external sense. But inside you can't be a whole, healthy person if you aren't true and just in your heart. That's pretty heavy stuff, and the Judge really gets a kick out of it. The time I spent with him didn't really seem like punishment. I can sure think of ways I'd rather spend my time, but he was pretty cool overall. And he said I could call him anytime I want if I have any questions. That doesn't sound likely, but it's good to know I can if I want.

After saying goodbye to the Judge, Ms. White showed up out of the blue, and said she'd heard from Mom that I needed to get hours on the road in order to take my driver's license test. Ms. White drives this little stick-shift Saturn sedan, and I've never used a clutch. We

spent forty-five minutes in the gym parking lot jerking around in circles until I got the hang of the clutch. Then we went out onto the
streets. It was a complete disaster. I kept stalling at stoplights or in
intersections, and folks were honking at us and glaring at us, and one
guy even gave us the finger. For some reason, the whole deal seemed
funny to Ms. White, and by the time the guy gave us the finger, she
was laughing so hard there were tears on her face. That started to
make me laugh too. Every time I'd start to screw it up again, she'd yell,
"And away we go!" and just crack up. After about an hour of this comedy routine, we got back to campus, and Ms. White jumped out of the
car, dropped to her knees, and kissed the pavement.

It was dinnertime in the Refectory for us boarders, and then a van
took us down to the Inner Harbor. After getting dropped off, we
screwed around for an hour or so until the movie time at 9:20. We saw
A Beautiful Mind. It was pretty cool seeing the guy who'd played the
Gladiator be a super-smart egghead. I also liked the way the movie
fooled you into thinking one way when that wasn't right at all. It gave
you a little taste of being nuts. The van picked us up, and we were back
on campus, with lights out, by midnight.

Today, I just watched football. The Ravens, only one year after
winning the Super Bowl, suck. I studied for a bunch of hours, and I
visited Mom at home.

Mr. Meader says I don't have to write as much in this journal,
which is a good thing. He says I have enough on my plate for the time
being. November's a crazy time, he tells me, here at St. Stephen's. This
week, we have something they call Manassas Creek Week. Manassas
Creek is a school in Virginia and our big arch-rival. All week we'll do
different stuff that the kids say is a lot of fun. Then the next week is
exam review week, and the week after that is end of trimester exams
before Thanksgiving break. Mr. Meader says I'll need all the time I can

get.

I don't know how much I'm going to get into all this stuff. My mood really goes back and forth. Sometimes I'm way down and worried about Mom and Stephie. Other times, things seem just normal. It's hard to predict how I'm going to feel about stuff at any given moment.

Chapter 12

Baltimore Sun Headlines, November 5-11

Taliban Winning Pakistan PR War

Africa is Seen as Ripe for Anthrax

President Warns of bin Laden Arms Bid

First Light of Ramadan

Tajikistan Embraces Alternatives to War

General Says U.S. Attacks on Track

Taliban City Falls to Rebels

Anthrax Killer Likely in U.S.;

Man With a Grudge, F.B.I. Says

U.S. Opposes Seizing of Kabul by Rebels

Quixotic Mission Against Taliban

JOURNAL ENTRY: NOVEMBER 11, 2001

We spent the whole day at home today. I slept until about ten, and then Mom, Stephie, and I had a huge brunch. Mom wore a bright turquoise bandana around her head. Her hair hadn't started falling out yet, but she nailed it with a "preemptive strike." She said she didn't want it coming out in her comb or clogging the drain in the shower, so she went to her hairdresser yesterday while I was at Mannassas Creek and had it all taken off. She even had her head waxed so light reflects off it! She still has her eyebrows, so with the bandana on, she doesn't look too weird. But her skin is sort of a gray, yellow color, and her eyes look sort of flat and dull. When she smiles, her eyes don't smile with her. She laid on the couch and read the paper while Stephie and I played Monopoly. The Ravens came on, and we watched some of that. Mom made nachos for us. I've got no homework because it's Mannassas Creek Weekend. That's a nice change!

It was a wild week at school. Every day a new banner made by some school organization would be hanging somewhere around school. There was, "Beat Mannassas Creek." There was a picture of a bull being cooked on a huge spit with an angel wearing a chef's cap getting ready to carve him up. We're the "Saints," and they're the "Bulls." "Make 'em run! NO Bull!" was my favorite. We did a school cheer at the end of chapel every morning, except for the day we had a special service about Ramadan. We were out of dress code all week long, so we all wore our game jerseys. The guys not on teams could just wear a shirt with the school colors.

On Friday night, we had a big cook-out. We ate these humongous steaks, which everybody calls "Bulloney," that they cooked outside on six charcoal grills. We had beans from a gigantic cauldron, and it's a tradition that everyone ladles himself a big scoop that he puts right on top of his steak. Then they give you a big sourdough roll that you're supposed to put on top of the beans. All of us—the whole faculty, staff, and students—ate sitting on the grass on the football field.

When it started to get dark, the littlest student in school walks by with this huge drum, and we all get up and follow him. We march behind him all around campus. He beats the drum and Pete, the student body president, walks right next to him, yelling into the electric megaphone, "Who are we?" The drum beats twice, and we all yell back, "We are the Saints!" The drum beats once, and Pete yells, "Who are they?" The drum beats twice, and we yell, "We don't know." The drum beats once, and Pete yells, "No Bull!" And the drum beats twice, and we yell back, "No Bull, No Bull!" It's really stupid, and it makes no sense at all, but everybody's doing it, and it's really fun. The noise is crazy. People are carrying the posters they made all week long. A bunch of seniors had torches, and it's getting dark fast. The drum starts to beat faster, and then some guy plays "charge" on a trumpet, and we all run, the whole school—teachers and Ms. White and everyone—to the parking lot, where there are no cars, just a huge pile of wood and two fire trucks. Just as we get there, a fireman lights the wood and it goes up in flames. Awesome!

There are five guys who have a band, and they're off to one side of the fire, and they start to jam, and the noise is great, and everybody's running in a circle around the fire. This goes on for awhile, and then the music suddenly stops. Pete has the microphone, and he gets us all to gather around. He leads us in a bunch of cheers, and I'm screaming like a crazy man just like everyone else. Then Ms. White takes the mike, and she reminds us that we'll eat breakfast together as a school tomorrow at 7:15 a.m. in the Refectory. We'll have a short chapel service at 7:45, and we'll be on the buses at 8:05 for the almost hour and forty-five minute bus ride to Mannassas Creek School. She then said that ice cream cones were available at the far end of the parking lot, and that this scene ended at 9:00 when everybody should head home for a good night's sleep. She then yelled, "Go Saints!" And the band went nuts again right on cue.

By 9:00 p.m., I was worn out from screaming and running around. I'm glad Mom decided for me to spend the whole week here. I could just stumble up to the third floor and crash. Morning seemed to show up about twenty minutes after I lay down. The breakfast at school was cool. Like that stupid cheer, the little guy with the drum, the beans in the cauldron, and the bonfire, breakfast was a tradition. We ate in total silence. Nobody said a word. There were gigantic pancakes and sausages. There were big pitchers of milk and O.J. on the table, and the varsity players waited on the tables. They've been doing breakfast this way for over a hundred years. Then Pete gets up and leaves and the seniors follow him out. The rest of us follow the seniors to the chapel, and the whole school sits there in silence.

Then the organ breaks the silence, and you practically get blown out of your seat with the first blasts of the school hymn. Everybody stands and sings. You never heard such a racket. Then we say the Lord's Prayer, and then after a moment's silence, Ms. White stands and says, "Let us pray." We all kneel, though some just sit, and she says,

"*Dear Lord, protect the boys of this school. Give them strength*
   to behave
With integrity, honor and courage. Give them the desire and
   the ability to
Act in accordance with your will, to behave with magnanimity,
   with kindness,
With dignity, with respect for others, with love for their fellow man.
Give them joy and pleasure in extending themselves, in pushing
   themselves,
In finding that which is best in themselves.
We ask this of you in the name of your only son, our savior,
   Jesus Christ. Amen."

Then Pete walks out of the chapel and onto one of the buses, and we all follow him. We have assigned buses by class, and we ride the whole way in a caravan of seven buses. Parents follow in their cars. It's cool. When we get there, it takes forever to get unloaded, because we get off one by one, one bus at a time. Your name is called. You go to the front of the bus, and waiting at the bottom of the steps is your host from the other school. They try to arrange it so your host is a guy you'll be playing against. Mine is a black kid named Kelvin from Tupelo, Mississippi. He's a halfback on the soccer team I'll be playing against. His job is to show me around the school, get me something to eat, and then take me to the gym to get ready for the game. Kelvin turns out to be a really good guy, and before I can give him any shit about the way he talks, he tells me I have the worst Yankee accent he ever heard. I'm telling you, this kid, Kelvin, has such a bad case of "south in the mouth." You can barely tell one word from the next because they all run together in one slow, drawn-out ooze of mispronounced vowels. It was great. He had me laughing all morning.

The school's awesome, and Kelvin says he really likes it. Like St. Stephen's, Mannassas Creek is older than God. It's a boarding school, though, and kids come from all over the country. Everything is made of light, pinkish brick, and every building has big white columns. They've got acres and acres of fields, not like us, where there's not much room in the city. He takes me into a place like our common room, where hot chocolate and doughnuts are being served. On all the walls in this big room, there's artwork by students. Almost half of the pictures are by St. Stephen's guys, and the other half are by Mannassas Creek students. Some of the stuff is really good.

Kelvin and I scarf about a dozen doughnuts together and we look at all the pictures for a while before he takes me over to his dorm and shows me his room. It's pretty cramped, and he says his roommate is a prick, but overall, he says it's not too bad, in spite of the fact that "the food really sucks." He calls it Yankee slop and that you have to get to Mississippi if you ever want to eat right. I tell him Virginia is the

South, and he gives me this weirded out look and says, "On whose map?"

At 11:00 we have to be at the gym. Our game starts at noon. All the third teams are already playing. They'll be done before we start. Then the varsity teams play at 3:15. The opposing varsity teams eat lunch together in their dining hall. It's an old tradition, like everything else about this weekend. They sit with the guy they'll be up against in the afternoon.

We lose our soccer game 2-1, but we play pretty well. I don't run into Kelvin much because he's on the other side of the field most of the time. After the game, he says he'll help me find a bite to eat before we break up to cheer for the varsity games. They're cooking burgers outside by the football field, and there's potato salad and apples and brownies and soda pop. Kelvin and I pig out.

It turns out they have a weak varsity soccer team this year, so it's not much of a game, but the football game is great. With only thirty seconds left on the clock, they kick off to us, and we nearly run it back for a TD. It gets all the way to their forty-yard line. We run out of time on their thirty, just a little out of range for our field goal kicker. They win 17-14 with a long field goal. Wow, it was a great game.

Then we go to chapel. Kelvin meets me at the door and we sit together. They have all sorts of extra chairs set up, but it's still really crowded. The chapel is brighter than ours. It's mostly white-painted wood, while ours is stone. The pews are all light oak, while ours are stained almost black. Our choir sings, and their choir sings. I think ours has got them beat by a lot, and then we pray. Their headmaster says some nice stuff about tradition and sportsmanship. Hell, that's all we talked about in chapel all last week. The same stuff—over and over—how you conduct yourself, representing your school, good sportsmanship, grace under pressure. Enough already!

Jake

We left there for dinner—a buffet. You could eat in the dining room, but if there wasn't enough room, you could sit in the common room, or anywhere else you felt like eating. I liked Kelvin more and more as I got to know him better. He has five older sisters, and he knew he had to get out of town when they tried to put him in a dress on his tenth birthday. He says they all treated him like he was their personal baby doll. Some nights, when he was real little, he said he had to take like four baths so they each could have a chance to wash the baby. They dressed him up and put him in a baby carriage and paraded him around town even after he was old enough to climb out and push the thing himself. He had me laughing so hard I thought I was going to croak.

When we finished eating, we all went into the auditorium for the night's program. The big event was the debate. The schools had three-man teams, which had been working for a month to prepare for the debate. St. Stephen's was the affirmative and had to support this statement: "RESOLVED, United States foreign policy is dominated by oil companies to the detriment of our national interests." Joel Kohn was the captain of our team, and we kicked major butt, though I have to admit that the other team was pretty hot, too. The kids on both teams all sounded like they could have been big time policy analysts. Afterward, the a capella singing groups from each school performed, and the Mannassas Creek guys had the edge on us. Maybe that's because our best singers are traditionally in the sacred music choir. The Mannassas Creek guys were really tight, and they had one guy with an awesome high voice—he was unreal.

At the end, there was an awards ceremony. Both schools had asked for volunteers to compete in a scholarly paper contest that was graded by a professor at the University of Virginia. The topic was to analyze the relative contributions of Adams and Jefferson to the successful formation of the United States. The paper could not exceed 10,000 words. That's a lot. Three guys from St. Stephen's participated and two from Mannassas Creek. The paper judged to be best was by a kid from Mannassas Creek who is from Korea. Go figure! We got the award for winning the debate, and we tied for first place in the juried art competition. All this stuff gets added to the sports records of the day, and it's totaled up in some formula. The school with the highest points wins the Founder's Cup and gets the school name engraved on the cup, which they get to take home for the next year. This has been going on forever.

Ms. White gets up near the lectern with their headmaster, who says, "As the host school, the privilege falls to me to announce this year's winner of the Founder's Cup. As you know, a school can be disqualified from the competition for receiving any unsportsmanlike conduct penalties during our athletic competitions, and on two sad and rare occasions in the history of this cup, we have declined to award the cup to either school. I am pleased to tell you that your conduct this year has been exemplary and both schools are qualified to receive the Founder's Cup. It falls then on the traditional formula to choose a winner, and in one of the tightest contests ever, for the second year in a row, Mannassas Creek School has earned the Founder's Cup."

At that point, everyone from St. Stephen's stood and applauded while the boys from Mannassas Creek remained seated. Tradition again. I found that a little hard to swallow, but there it is.

While we are clapping, they all stand and begin to leave. When they're gone, we start out, and it takes forever to get out of the room. Their whole school, starting outside of the front door, is lined up. Each guy holds a lighted candle, and we shake hands with every one of them all the way down their long walkway to where the buses are parked. Then we get on the buses and leave. I slept the whole way back.

It was 11:30 when we pulled into St. Stephen's. Mom was there waiting for me. Steph too, even though it was so late. We drove home as a family.

Chapter 13

Baltimore Sun Headlines, November 12-18

Afghans in Exile Consider Future

Allies Seeking Taliban's Successor

Pentagon to Beef Up Presence in Region

Nuclear Warhead Cutback Pledged

Taliban Frees Aid Workers

Pashtun Rising in the South, U.S. Says

Military Advisers Expand Activity

Longtime Foes Revive Struggle for Power

NOVEMBER 12, 2001—CHAPEL TALK,
DELIVERED BY RECTOR MARY WHITE

Congratulations to all of you on a fine Mannassas Creek Weekend. Not only did our athletes, artists, debaters, scholars, and singers represent our school wonderfully well, our fans conducted themselves with dignity and sportsmanship. The spirit you showed, in the week leading up to the game, was fun and appropriate. I am very proud of you.

This week is review week, and I know that the workload is intense. Our traditional Turkey Bowl draft occurs today, and tomorrow we will post the teams. This is an old tradition here at school and a healthy way to blow off steam. You will be free to leave school at the conclusion of your Turkey Bowl competition every day at about 5:00 p.m. Dinner will be available in the Refectory at 5:30, and teachers will be in their offices from 6:00 p.m. to 8:00 p.m. for any student seeking extra help. You will not receive new material this week, but you may be asked to complete work sheets, write essays, or take quizzes and tests designed to help you master material already covered. We believe that cultivating students' ability to synthesize and internalize large amounts of material not only helps them retain information but also fosters in them the skill of working under time constraints to produce quality work that they will need for the rest of their lives.

I want to take some extra time here in chapel today to explain a school policy that some feel is antiquated and no longer useful, and also to explain a decision I have reached in applying that policy. My subject is the Athletic Competition Policy as applied to our basketball players' desire this year to play in two Christmas tournaments.

Since I believe that our Athletic Competition Policy remains appropriate and consistent with our school mission, I tested my conviction by making that policy the central point of discussion during our October Board of Trustees meeting. The Board unanimously affirmed our policy, but they also delegated to me the authority to make exceptions on a case-by-case basis under extraordinary circumstances that do not undermine the mission of our school.

Since many of you, and also many of your parents, question our policy, I want to spend time this morning, when we are between athletic seasons, to explain it to you. A copy of this explanation will be sent home to your parents.

Our Athletic Competition Policy states that no St. Stephen's team will practice or play games during school vacations or on Sundays. No team may practice for longer than two hours on any given day, and practices most often should be under one hour and a half. We will not participate in post-season play or playoffs except as our league dictates that we must. Our sports seasons will not overlap. We will not travel farther than one hour from Baltimore to play a game, except for the Mannassas Creek Weekend, every other year. Athletics will not be allowed to infringe upon the normal academic day, and students may not miss classes for athletic contests.

We believe in athletics as a critical component of our school's mission. We believe that competition in the venue of sports helps students develop physical fitness, confidence, discipline, selflessness, self-control, and intensity of focus. It allows students to practice qualities of courage, grace under pressure, and resistance to fatigue. Athletics provide an arena of urgency where lessons are immediate, concrete, and unforgettable. Students must learn how to properly internalize the elation of success and the disappointment of failure. Students learn the dynamics of a team, how to cooperate, to sublimate personal interests for the sake of a greater good. And, of course, let us not forget that athletics are supposed to be fun, a freeing and joyous antidote to the sometimes pressured and sedentary academic day.

Given our strong belief in the positive place for athletics within our school mission, why do we insist upon retaining our Athletic Competition Policy? We believe that, at many other schools, sports have become the tail that wags the dog. Many schools practice sports informally all summer long, and most schools in our league begin formal practice in early August. Most schools also practice and play over both Christmas and Spring vacations. Schools routinely practice and play on both Saturdays and Sundays. Most schools, by their actual policies, if not by their words and intentions, have encouraged specialization. A true three-sport athlete at most schools would have, at most, a total of thirty days a year away from adult-sponsored sports teams. At these schools, athletics routinely infringe upon the academic day and make it very difficult for athletes to participate fully in the life of the school. They simply do not have enough time to be in the school play, to sing in the choir, to be on the debate team.

Our society seems to have confused excellence with winning championships. Playoffs, tournaments, and post-season play have arrived at schools by an interesting route. They were once non-existent. Most athletics at schools were intramural. When interscholastic competition became the norm, there were regular seasons and no championship playoffs or special tournaments to crown the best. But money changed all that. The pros began to dominate sports after World War II, and more and more elaborate ways to capture an audience were developed. Then came TV, and now everybody makes the playoffs except the poor fellows in last place. The regular season has become almost irrelevant. The seasons are no longer limited. In one form or another, they stretch interminably throughout the year. I do not suppose that there is anything inherently wrong with all of this at the professional level, but let us not forget that it has nothing to do with producing excellence or promoting values. It has everything to do with money.

Before long, colleges and universities began to ape the pros. A former president of Princeton University recently wrote a book called *The Game of Life* that tries to illustrate the significant impact of athletics on institutions of higher learning.

And then came schools like ours, which also began aping the pros. Hopeful parents see athletics not as worthwhile for their own value, but as tickets to some other destination. Athletics are being allowed to infringe upon every other area of school life. In the noise of glory and championships, and in the hope for fame or money or both, we have lost sight of their inherent, quiet value.

We, at St. Stephen's, are not going there. We have successfully resisted the pull to worship at the altar of professional athletics, and we will continue to do so. Nonetheless, five boys approached me in September with a respectful and reasoned argument that an exception should be made. They have been invited to play in holiday basketball tournaments in both Washington and Philadelphia. I have agreed to make an exception to the policy so that they may play in only one of the two tournaments, with the explicit understanding that this is an *exception* to policy, not a *change* in policy.

Why the exception? Circumstances, in my view, have conspired to make this exception wise, although any one or two of these circumstances alone would not have been enough. I will not elaborate in great detail, but I do want to explain my reasoning.

First, the five seniors, two of whom have started on the varsity since their ninth grade year, and the other three, who have started on the varsity since their tenth grade year, approached me properly. They did not challenge the policy itself, but merely asked for an exception. They did not try to stir up emotions, but dealt with me in private, stating that they would abide by my decision regardless of what it was.

Second, these boys are all scholars first. One has committed to Stanford and another to Princeton. A third has applied early decision to Williams College because of that institution's superb Art History program, and he reasonably expects to be admitted. The fourth and fifth are having difficulty deciding between Duke, Georgetown, and Penn. They all take academics seriously. They all have honors averages.

Third, these boys joined a rich basketball tradition when they arrived. We have several graduates playing Division I college basketball, and we have two graduates in the NBA. Our coach has been here for twenty-five years, and we are known for ferocious man-to-man defense á la Indiana, and a disciplined, cutting back-door offense, with great three-point shooting á la Princeton. You all know what a big fan

I am, as a former J.V. coach here at St. Stephen's and a veteran of many wonderful cheering seasons. But even with this great tradition, these boys have taken us to a different, higher level. They were not challenged last year by any school in this area—public, independent or parochial. They simply have no local competition. I do not expect that we will see a team quite like this one any time soon.

Fourth, these boys are not specialists. One, Tyrone is our star soccer goalie, and an excellent first baseman, who sings in the choir. Another, James, is on the debate team, plays defensive back on the football team, and is a superb sprinter in the spring. A third, Darnell, is our most accomplished artist, a tight end in football, and a spring-time shot-put and discus man. Fourth, in Jamal, we have the state high-jumping champion, cross country runner, jazz pianist, and school comedian. Finally, in Andrew, we have the high-scoring striker, baseball shortstop, and math team captain. This is a rare collection of boys gathered in a single class.

Fifth, these boys have not received a single technical foul for unsportsmanlike behavior in three years. They have been superb sportsmen. They represent our school spectacularly.

All five of these circumstances, taken as a whole, convince me that in this rare confluence of events, an exception is warranted. The boys will be going to Philadelphia.

Please do not misunderstand me. Our policy is unchanged, but policies cannot be completely rigid or they lose the force of persuasion and become a source of anger and division. I'm proud of these boys. They represent the best of our school in mind, body, and spirit.

But guess what follows?! You still can't practice until after Thanksgiving break. Good luck in the Turkey Bowl! Good luck with review and with your exams!

Jake

This week is nuts. I'm staying up all night. How could review be even tougher than regular school? We have a ton of stuff to turn in because of the huge supplementary reading assignments. We have about forty math problems every night. The only good thing has been the Turkey Bowl. We all play touch football, and the faculty are the refs. It's a gas.

Mom picked me up every night at 8:00 when review and extra help sessions end. She is looking pretty awful, to say the least, and I heard her puking last night. She never complains, though, and she picks me up and takes me to school every day. Yesterday, we went for a three-hour drive, and while I practiced on the country roads all the way up into Pennsylvania, she fell asleep.

I think I'm ready for exams. I've worked my ass off.

Chapter 14

Baltimore Sun Headlines, November 19-25

Secret Anti-terror Court at Issue
Tribunal 'Absolute Right Thing'
Afghanistan Factions OK Power Talks
Bush Vows Terror Fight Will Go On
Dogs Go Back to Finding Miner
Anthrax Claims a 5th Victim
Jab, Feint, Pause, Then Calm in Kunduz
Pakistani Spies Long Linked to Militants
Taliban Giving Up Kunduz

JOURNAL ENTRY: NOVEMBER 25, 2001

I've needed this break. I've pretty much just eaten, slept, and watched the tube during the entire Thanksgiving vacation. Yesterday was sort of cool and weird at the same time. In the morning, Mom and Stephie were passengers as I drove all over Baltimore County. After stopping over in Monkton by an old railroad path, we took a real slow walk along the Gunpowder in a place where Hank, my old partner, and I used to ride our dirt bikes. We talked about all sorts of stuff, and believe it or not, I convinced Mom to go fishing with me. She had to take a nap after we got back home at lunch time, so I made

Jake

Stephie and me some bologna sandwiches, and I went up in the attic to find some of the gear I knew was stored up there. Some of it is pretty moldy and nasty, but I found a pair of boot-foot waders that I hosed off. They're patched in places but look good. I rigged up an old Leonard five-weight for Mom, with some extra double taper light-green floating line I had lying around that went onto a Pflueger reel that looked twenty-five years old. It wasn't exactly a perfect set-up, but I thought it would work. Not enough backing-line if she hooks a big one, but that won't happen today. She says she wants to fish on the surface, but the big ones are lying low and deep.

When Mom got up, she felt a little queasy, but by 3:00 she was feeling good enough that we drove over to York Road, where there's a little park and real easy shallow wading on the Gunpowder. Stephie messed around with some toys at a picnic table while Mom and me stepped into the water.

I didn't want her to know I was watching her, but I was real curious about how Mom would do. I've never seen her fish. She fished for crappie and bass with Pops when she was a little girl, and she told me about how she and Dad fished for trout on their honeymoon out on the Madison and Gallatin rivers in Montana and Wyoming. They fished at least once a week all year-round on the Gunpowder and Western Run before I was born. She hadn't picked up a rod since Dad was killed.

I went around a slight bend in the river, where I could still watch Mom and cast upstream and across current. She waded out real, real slow, leaning on a wading staff I'd given her, to a spot on a gravel bar only about ankle deep. Then she just stood there completely motionless like a great blue heron. She didn't even twitch for maybe five minutes. Then she looked down at her hand with the rod in it, like she'd just remembered why she was there. She stripped a little line off the reel and shook some line out of the rod tip and let it float past her. The line straightened, and she lifted it off the water with an easy bend of her elbow. Then she sent a small, tight loop straight behind her before making a quick arm-straightening move forward that sent the line quartering upstream about thirty feet out. As the #12 Adams floated downstream, she stripped the line in, and then she did this neat little sideways roll cast that just flicked the fly back up stream without drawing the line back in a casting motion. She definitely knows what she's doing. Now I'm a little worried about not putting enough backing on the line.

After about thirty minutes, she was exhausted. I watched as she slowly sloshed back across the river from her gravel bar. She looked small and old in those baggy patched waders, and her silly orange bandana flapping in the wind (she chose day-glo orange for fishing, who knows why?). Her eyebrows and eyelashes are gone now. She has a sore throat all the time, she wears a little white mask when she's out in public because her immune system is weak, and she also wears these little gold earrings or these gold hoops. Coming downstairs yesterday with her bandana off and only one hoop in, she said she was Mr. Clean. Since I didn't know who Mr. Clean was, I didn't get the joke.

Anyway, she sat in the sun with Stephie while I fished for another hour. It's not usually this sunny and warm in late November, but this day felt like April. There was even a little hatch coming off the water, some midges of some kind, and I saw a few splashy rises of small fish near the bank. No luck, though. It was strange to have Mom, looking like a miniature day-glo pirate, out on the river with me. Who would have guessed she was an expert? Afterward, we all went home, Mom lay down on the couch, and Stephie and I watched football and played crazy eights. We ordered-in pizza and ate that for dinner. Mom doesn't usually go for that order-in stuff, but she's got to chill out until she gets her energy back.

Exams were on the Monday, Tuesday, and Wednesday before Thanksgiving, and they were brutal. I have no idea how I did. We'll get the results back on Tuesday. They give us the day off tomorrow so the teachers can finish grading, and I'm going to fish all day. All the exams were over by 12:30 on Wednesday, and after them we had a Thanksgiving Convocation. Different people from the school—secretaries, maintenance guys, students, teachers, and alumni—all spoke real briefly about what they were thankful for this year. One lady cried while she said how thankful she was for her baby, who was born prematurely and who only recently came home from the hospital, six weeks after his birth. A little Asian man who I see driving the tractor around school spoke so you could hardly understand him, but you got the point that he was grateful to be in a place where he could be free. Ms. White finished up, and she asked us for a moment of silence in remembrance of the people who died on September 11th and the men who are serving our country in Afghanistan. All in all, it was pretty moving stuff.

After the service, we had the fall banquet. It was roast beef, since everybody would eat turkey the next day. Coaches talked about their teams and handed out letters. Most Valuable Player awards were given out. Best fall debater awards, best painting in the fall art show, best this and best that—all got handed out. It wasn't bad because nobody spoke for too long and the food was good. I was real sleepy, though, and might have liked it better at another time.

Mom picked me up at 3:30 p.m. and we went grocery shopping for Thanksgiving dinner. We only needed a small Butterball turkey this year for just the three of us—no guests. We didn't buy any of those God-awful creamed onions and none of those make-you-gag turnips. Just mashed potatoes, green beans, stuffing, and cranberry sauce.

Breyer's vanilla ice cream and chocolate sauce, too. By the time we finished walking around the store, Mom looked real wobbly. She sat down by the door while I checked out the food. It's the first time I ever used an automatic paying machine by myself, where you swipe a credit card through a slot. Pretty cool. I had never really checked out how much food costs, never paid any attention. I was surprised that one lousy little meal would cost so much. Mom said that she usually buys in bulk at Sam's Club or Price Club or somewhere she can get a discount, but it was just too much hassle today.

We cooked the stuff together. Mom pretty much sat at the kitchen table, peeled potatoes, and gave directions. Stephie is a better cook than I am, which is a little embarrassing. She and Mom were laughing at me because I didn't know where anything was and didn't even know how to set the oven temperature. That's stuff I need to know, and I am one sorry dude in the food preparation world. It all came out pretty well. Stephie did pretty well, but Mom just can't take much food. She says sometimes even the smell upsets her stomach. I ate one whole half of the turkey. I think it's a tradition that you eat until you think you'll pop. I just lay on my back in the living room until I felt better. Stephie lay there right next to me. Mom lay on the couch. And all three of us fell asleep like a trio of corpses laid out on slabs. We cleaned up later in the day.

That's enough. I'll fish tomorrow. Then we start the second trimester. I feel fresher than I have in a while.

Chapter 15

Baltimore Sun Headlines, November 26-December 2
Afghan Women Slowly Embrace New Freedom
Kunduz Falls Amid Looting, Chaos
Marines Dig In, Jets Attack
Cloned Human Embryos Draw Focus, Fire
Bush Deems 'Evil' a Good Word to Use
Jets Target Taliban Compounds
CIA Officer Died in Jail Revolt
Last Stronghold of Taliban in Peril
Bombs Kill at Least 10 in Israel
Planes Pound Taliban Redoubt

NOVEMBER 29, 2001—COVER LETTER TO ALL PARENTS
FROM RECTOR MARY WHITE

Dear Karen:

You will find enclosed with this letter what we call our first trimester summary packet. On top is a data sheet, followed by a letter from your son's advisor, followed by course coverage descriptions, followed by a grade sheet, and concluded by teacher comments. These materials should give you a thorough sense of your son's work and standing during this academic year's first trimester. If you have any questions, please call your son's advisor first. He will either answer your question or direct you to someone who can.

Despite the tragic start to this academic year, I am pleased with the tone of our school. The senior class has provided us with good examples of fine citizenship and has led the student body admirably. I am particularly pleased by the thoughtful and provocative senior chapel talks we have been blessed to hear. Our accomplishments in the community service arena continue to benefit the city of Baltimore in areas of soup kitchen support, tutoring disadvantaged youngsters, environmental clean-up, work with the mentally handicapped, and care for the elderly. St. Stephen's boys are having a positive impact all over the city, not only during their required Saturday service days but on every day of the week. We are very proud of our students' enthusiastic embrace of a service ethic.

Our winter trimester is a little scattered as a result of multiple interruptions to the academic routine, the longest of which is Christmas break. We have three full weeks of classes before that wonderfully long respite, but even those consecutive weeks are made particularly full by our holiday concerts and festivities. Please do participate in our celebrations as often as your family schedule permits, and do remember that these special events are required appointments for all our students. We do not permit students to depart early for vacation except under emergency circumstances, so please do not ask us to release your sons before their last school appointment on Friday, December 21.

Let me take this opportunity to thank you once again for sharing your delightful sons with us. We are proud to have them at St. Stephen's and are grateful for the energy, talent, and spirit that make our school such a healthy, vibrant place. Let me also publicly say a word of thanks to our extraordinary teachers. This collection of dedicated men and women are a gift to their students, and I am more grateful than I can adequately express for the services they render to us all.

Sincerely,

Mary White

Rector, St. Stephen's Episcopal School

HANDWRITTEN NOTE ON BOTTOM OF
RECTOR WHITE'S COVER LETTER

Karen,

Amongst the trials and tribulations of your daunting physical challenge, I hope you can draw strength and pleasure from the huge strides that Jake has made during his short time with us. The comments about him reflect genuine, remarkable growth. I hope it is not unfair to observe that he arrived at St. Stephen's plunged in adolescent self-absorption. He seems to be surfacing from these depths. His effort is strong in every area, and his results will improve as he becomes accustomed to our school's peculiarities. Jake has also reacted remarkably well to the consequences of his honor violation. I believe he has genuinely learned and grown from that mistake. Please do not hesitate to call me with any questions or concerns that you may have.

Mary

MR. MEADER'S ADVISOR LETTER, DATED NOVEMBER 28, 2001

Dear Mrs. Collins:

It pleases me tremendously to see a student progress so quickly at St. Stephen's. The difficulties that new tenth graders face are considerable. They have not enjoyed the advantage of our ninth grade program, which helps youngsters adjust to our school's pace and rigor. Nonetheless, Jake seems to have made the transition after some early fits and starts.

At the outset, he seemed reluctant to participate fully in the life of the school. St. Stephen's seemed to be a necessary evil to be tolerated, not an opportunity to be grasped. Initially, he was quiet in class and went through the motions in community service and around campus. Only on the soccer field did he show any spark or sense of enthusiasm. He was in no way objectionable, just disengaged and perhaps a little self-absorbed. Some boys make an art form out of flying just below the radar, and Jake looked at the outset as if he may have had experience practicing that skill.

On the academic side, Jake has struggled with the writing demands of our Humanities program. He was unfamiliar with a five paragraph expository essay, and his writing tended to be a regurgitation of facts rather than an analysis or an argument. With help from the Study Skills Department, he has made significant improvement in this area. He also seems to be studying more efficiently and taking notes more effectively.

Jake has real science and math aptitude, as you will see from his teachers' comments. I have urged Jake to take some intellectual risks. He seems to play it safe and excels in areas that are objective and have been reviewed in class. When teachers ask him to theorize or apply learned principles to new and unfamiliar problems, he hesitates and

Jake

holds back.

Outside of the classroom, Jake has been an enthusiastic soccer player, but at the start only a reluctant and even a slightly sullen participant in our Saturday Community Service Program. I am pleased to report that he has really turned himself around in our Environmental Club and appears to enjoy our Jones Falls Watershed Projects.

Without dwelling too long on Jake's honor violation, since we have talked exhaustively about that subject, I will repeat only that Jake's honesty after the mistake and his subsequent willing and good-humored acceptance of the consequences have been truly heartening. I do believe that mistake was a one-time aberration.

Jake reports that you are recovering well from your operation. You have our support, and I hope you know that we want to be helpful in any way we can. With regard to Jake, I believe his talks with the school counselor have been useful. He was angry about the situation at the outset, and he clammed up and wouldn't talk to anyone about his feelings. He has opened up in the last little while, and he seems to be more philosophical. Although I think he actually enjoyed his time in the dormitory, he expressed to me real pleasure at the prospect of going home. My sense is that he has gained some equilibrium after the initial shock of your situation, and now he remains fearful but calm. Please let me know if his words or actions suggest that he needs any special attention from our end.

In summary, Jake has settled in here well despite some significant challenges, both academic and personal. His grades are good for the first trimester at St. Stephen's, so do not let him panic about the report card. I know he has never received anything less than an "A," but it is only the rarest of students who achieves anything close to that at St. Stephen's. The lone "D" in Humanities would be a "C" absent the "zero" Jake received for the honor violation. I enjoy having Jake as an advisee and look forward to the growth of our relationship over the coming year.

Sincerely,
George Meader

FIRST TRIMESTER REPORT FOR JAKE PHILLIPS:

Course	Teacher	Grade
Humanities*	Marks/Smith	D
Geometry	Meader	B
Physics	Hanson	B
French II	Saunders	C

*Humanities is reported twice on our official transcript as English and AP Modern European History. It is a double period course taught by a teacher from the English Department and a teacher from the History Department, along with lecturers from the Art, Music, and Religion Departments.

Sport: Third Team Soccer
Community Service: Environmental Club

TEACHER COMMENTS

Humanities—Kathleen Marks and Jerry Smith

Jake started slowly in our class, but then accelerated to a satisfactory level of work. But for his honor violation, his grade would have been a solid "C," so please do not be overly concerned with his "D" grade.

We are particularly pleased with Jake's effort. Because he was so reticent in class, it was difficult to tell at the start of the term whether he was truly engaged with his academic work. From the beginning, however, he rarely failed to answer correctly an objective question. He has always come to class prepared, and his level of effort has been commendable.

His difficulties seem to lie in the skills area. His writing is improving, but his early essays demonstrated an unfamiliarity with the expository essay format. He had trouble building a satisfactory introductory paragraph with a clear thesis. He preferred to list facts without making sense of them or supporting a perspective. He substituted bare assertions for reasoned, supported argument, and he failed to adequately explain conclusions he had reached.

Jake also did not have good note-taking skills, and we discovered that his approach to his homework assignments was inefficient. Jake was wasting time and spinning his wheels. Thanks to help from our study skills specialist, we have seen significant progress in these areas, and we are hopeful that Jake will see improved grades as a tangible result.

Finally, we are pleased that Jake has abandoned his initial reserve, and despite his worry over your health, has become an engaged and interested member of the class.

Geometry—George Meader

Jake is a talented mathematics student who has done honors work from the start of the year. He memorizes all the formulas, theorems, and algebraic equations necessary for successful work in geometry, and he turns in flawless homework assignments. He is separated from our top mathematics students only by his hesitance "to think outside the box." All our tests have a section, which is roughly fifteen percent of the grade, that tests our students' ability to apply principles we have covered to material that is unfamiliar or new. Students must "noodle around" or think creatively about the problem and suggest ways it can be approached, even if they cannot find a solution. They might be called brainteasers, and we aim to provoke students into "thinking like mathematicians." Mathematics is, among other things, a creative exercise of the mind. Arriving at elegant solutions to complicated problems with multiple variables is where Jake gets tripped up. He becomes frustrated with the material and with me, and even voiced his sense—and a common student complaint—that it is "unfair" to test a student on material he has not studied. Despite this frustration, I can see progress in Jake's thinking and believe he will get the hang of thinking "like a mathematician."

Physics—Bill Hanson

Jake gets Physics. He has a knack for it. His home works are complete, thorough, and accurate. His labs are detailed and careful. He pays excellent attention to detail. Jake's weakness is his writing. He is getting help from our study skills people, and I have seen improvement. Jake's essays, summaries, and reports are often disorganized. He needs improvement in stating a clear thesis in clear declarative sentences, and then supporting that thesis without digressing. I am confident that Jake will improve even more in his writing skills. They are the only thing that separates him from our top students. Parenthetically, Jake's continued good work while concerned with his mom is a tribute to his strength of character. I wish him and his family well.

Jake

French II—Helen Saunders

Jake memorizes his vocabulary. He learns his grammar. His homework is always complete. All this is good, but I cannot get him to speak. If he will speak in French, participate in class, and dare to seem a little foolish, his performance will improve. Jake seems to tolerate this class as a necessary evil, and this does not promote his success. I admire very much his continued solid performance in the face of his fears over his mother's health, and I hope to be helpful in any way I can.

JOURNAL ENTRY: DECEMBER 2, 2001

Grades and comments are in. You'd think I was doing OK from the comments, except maybe French, but anybody at my old school who got grades like that would be about three IQ points away from a monkey. I got two Bs, a D, and a C—that gives me a C average. A "C" is what they call good work, and they claim it puts me right in the middle of the class. Mr. Meader said I should chill out and not worry about the grades. He says I'm doing fine. Mom says the same thing. I'm not buying it. I can't work any harder than I am now. If this study skills stuff and this extra help I go for doesn't pay off next trimester, I don't know what I'll do. I don't want to beat my brains out and see no results. I knew I wasn't going to be number one in the class, but I never thought I'd wind up being a guy with a "C" average and a "D" on my report card.

Mom has been picking me up every day at about 6:00. I can't believe she started back at work on Thursday. She goes in for half a day, and when she picked me up Thursday night, she looked about the color of an overcooked lima bean. I drove home, and she fell asleep almost the second her butt hit the passenger seat. I'm not sure it's so smart to go to work so soon after the operation, and while she's trying to make it thorough all those treatments. She's got to feel like shit. Stephie and I have been making dinner while she gives directions from the kitchen table. She doesn't complain at all. Stephie looks real worried all the time and tries to act like a little nurse. She tries hard to be helpful, but I think she causes Mom to spend more energy than she would without the help. Stephie reads out loud to her, and fluffs her pillow on the couch, and asks her if she needs something about every thirty seconds. I tried to get her to back off, but when she was out of the room, Mom said, "Let her do it, Jake. It's important for her. She's really scared, doesn't understand all of this, and needs to feel helpful. Let her be. I'm fine."

We had basketball try-outs on Tuesday, Wednesday, and Thursday. There were way too many guys for the three teams, and on Friday I got cut. I could see it coming. They don't need a short point guard who can't dribble and can't shoot. You should see the varsity guys play. Unbelievable. It's like watching the NBA. There are two guys who can jam behind their heads, and I watched this one guy hit eight straight threes from what seemed like half court. They get up and down the court so fast, you can hardly believe it. They press full court, either man-to-man, or with a trap at half court. It's going to be fun watching these guys play.

I'll play intramural basketball. The school has a six-team league with eight or nine guys on each team. A teacher is assigned as a coach to each team, and a draft is held to see who is on which team. They apparently use the same system as the school's varsity team and run skills clinics for us. We'll practice three days a week and play twice a week. We get uniforms and real officials at every game, and people take the league real seriously. We have a championship, and an all-star team plays the faculty in front of the whole school just before spring break. It sounds pretty cool.

The academic grind is back on. I'm busy.

Chapter 16

Baltimore Sun Headlines, December 3-9

Hamas Strikes Israel Again

U.S. Warplanes Pound Kandahar as Noose Tightens

Israelis Avenge Attacks, Hit Arafat's Compound

Taliban Stalling Marine Advance on Kandahar

American Captured Fighting for Taliban

'Friendly Fire' Kills 3 U.S. Troops

Taliban to Surrender Kandahar

Taliban Abandon Kandahar

U.S. Forces Seek Enemy Commanders

DECEMBER 3, 2001—CHAPEL TALK,
DELIVERED BY RECTOR MARY WHITE

This is a sad and difficult moment for me. I stand before you today to report about the single most unpleasant and unhappy moment in the life of a school—the expulsion of a student. In this case, it is three students. Worst of all, all three boys were seniors who were spending their fourth year with us. They violated the honor code in an egregious way and then lied about their actions. Nothing gives me, your rector, and your teachers more personal anguish and sense of abject failure than when we do not persuade our students about the importance of honesty, of personal integrity. How did we fail them? Why couldn't we reach them? Why didn't we notice that our school mission was not influencing them? As your faculty, we have open and honest meetings of self-examination during which we try to understand where we went wrong.

But even as we feel personal failure, our disappointment in the boys themselves is acute. Each one of us is ultimately responsible for his own integrity and honor. We cannot blame others when we fail. We grow and learn from our errors only when we assume full responsibility for our actions. So these boys are suffering the consequences of their premeditated and calculated actions. They are responsible and accountable and have therefore been separated from St. Stephen's School.

Two of those senior boys managed to hack into Advanced Placement Calculus computer files. This was a dubious but precocious accomplishment, as they had to overcome a wide variety of firewalls and fail-safes set up by our school computer consultants. If they had spent even a small percentage of the time they wasted in cracking our system in studying for the Calculus test, they would have fared rather well. Whatever their reasons, they persisted in their efforts to beat our system, and they succeeded. Having downloaded the Math Department's AP Calculus examination, they told a third boy of their feat, explaining to him what they had done and how they had accomplished it. This boy actually visited the Math Department files himself, and browsed around some, but apparently downloaded nothing. He told the other boys that he had broken in, too, and that what they had done was "really cool," but for reasons that were not entirely clear even to him, he refused to look at the Calculus examination.

The chair of our Technology Department realized that the school computer files had been compromised by two unauthorized entries. He successfully discovered which school terminals had been used to break into the Math Department, and he reported the break-in to the chair of the Math Department.

The Math Department then convened a meeting, where it was decided to keep all the examinations the same except to switch some small part of every problem, either a variable, a number, or a sine. Two examinations were submitted by two boys under their honor pledge that had answers consistent with the original exam, but that were glaringly flawed for the revised exam. When confronted, they professed their innocence. In desperation and in obvious collaboration with one another, they tried to place the blame on the third boy. The third boy was then confronted, and he lied to the teachers, to the chair of the Honor Committee, and then to the Honor Committee itself. When he realized what deep trouble he was in, he decided to tell the truth. It was, frankly, too little, too late. Even though he had not cheated on the exam, he knew about it, actually encouraged it with admiration and enthusiasm, did nothing to stop it, either with the two boys themselves or with any other member of the community, and then lied about it on several separate occasions.

I don't believe any of you doubt that what these boys did was wrong. Some of you may wonder why we resorted to expulsion. How, you might ask, can a school that claims to be a family, that states its love and care for its students, throw them out on the street? After all, a loving parent does not merely abandon his or her child when the child makes a terrible mistake. On the contrary, the parent must work even harder to help the child. Isn't the school hypocritical in abandoning a student?

That question cannot be dismissed cavalierly. I, your teachers, and the Board of Trustees take it very seriously. And the answer is not

entirely clear-cut. It has to do with a balance. What are the best interests of the boy, and what are the best interests of the school community? If an action is flagrant and serious enough that tolerating it would
undermine our ability to say honestly that we take honor or integrity
seriously, we believe that expulsion must be considered. We believe
that tolerance of the actions in this case would undermine our mission
and support the notion that we do not take seriously issues surrounding honor and integrity. We would lose our institutional credibility
with you, the students.

On the best interests of the student side of the equation, it is
important to remember that at St. Stephen's, unlike membership in a
conjugal family, membership is a privilege, not a right. Every student
joins our school community with the clear understanding that the privilege can be revoked for failure to adhere to our fundamental principles. A student who leaves St. Stephen's can go to another school, can
graduate from that school, and can attend college. Expulsion is very
serious and painful, but it is not a permanent condemnation.
However, it *is* a serious consequence for a serious wrong. It supports
the idea of personal responsibility. A boy who can stare his mistake in
the eye, blame no one but himself, and accept the consequences of his
action, is a boy who will be better off for the expulsion. Sometimes the
only sure way to educate or change some boys is for them to fall hard.
Only then can they rise transformed.

In this rational explanation, there is very little comfort, because
we are dealing with friends about whom we care deeply. If you are
upset about these expulsions, please know that your teachers and I
join you. If you feel the decision is unfair, or wrong, feel free to speak
with any senior class officer, any teacher, your advisor, or me.
Sometimes it is not possible to agree on a decision, but at least we can,
as people of good faith, understand and respect one another's deci-

sions.

I regret very much having to give you this sad news today, and I hope you will join me in wishing these expelled boys our strongest hopes for their future success and happiness.

JOURNAL ENTRY: DECEMBER 9, 2001

Work is a bear as usual, but I got a B on a Humanities five paragraph expository essay. That's a first! Intramural hoops is a gas. The teachers are really into it, and we play really hard. I think I actually might be getting better.

Joel was doing one of his singing things the whole time we took water samples yesterday. He's nuts! You could hear him above the traffic on the expressway singing "In the jungle . . ." complete with this squeaky falsetto "weem-a-wacka, weem-a-wacka" chorus.

Mom took me out driving afterwards, and she is definitely not looking good. She leaned her head up against the passenger side window and just stared ahead for the whole hour. She insisted on cooking me and Stephie dinner, which was spaghetti, and then she watched us eat while she sipped on a glass of water. She never complains. She goes to work, goes grocery shopping, gets her treatment, sleeps, eats sometimes, and takes care of us. She must be one tough lady, given what I can see she's going through and given what those chemicals and the radiation do to her body.

Ms. White called me into her office on Wednesday and asked about Mom. She told me how incredible Mom is just for doing what she's doing. I gather that Mom came into school a little early on Saturday before picking me up and had a long talk with Ms. White. They seemed to hit it off pretty good. I get nervous when my mother hangs around too much with the principal, but I can't think of any-

him but couldn't find him in the dark. Then on Saturday, an early morning fisherman spotted him standing upright in the bottom of the pool with the top of his head just below the surface of the water. He had drowned. They figure he stepped into the hole not realizing how deep it was, and his waders filled up with water.

The article on him was long. He'd retired from Legg Mason about four years ago and was from an old prominent Baltimore family. He owned horses, and a bunch of them had won the Maryland Hunt Cup. He rode in it a couple of times himself but never won. He'd been a fighter pilot in the Pacific during World War II. They say he was survived by a wife of fifty-two years, three children, and seven grandchildren. He loved to fish, mostly out west and in Argentina, but his favorite place in the world, according to the article, was a friend's farm along Western Run on summer evenings, when the sulfur hatch was on and the big browns came up off the bottom to slurp the mayflies down. He was a member of the Maryland Club, the Elkridge Club, the Greenspring Valley Hunt Club, and St. George's Church. That's our church, but I didn't know him.

It was kinda spooky to see him dead on the bank and then to read that nice article about him. Once you've seen a corpse that you never saw alive, it's hard to picture him fishing and riding horses and walking around Baltimore. I couldn't help but think about the guy we found in the Jones Falls during the Environmental Club clean-up. There was no article on him. I looked every day for a week. Nothing. Maybe they couldn't figure out who he was. Maybe they just didn't think he was important enough to mention. But both guys looked the same. That really stands out to me. When you're dead, you're the same as other dead guys.

Spring break came not one second too soon. I was just about dead. They said that the winter trimester would be different, and it was, but it was the same endless work. I handled it without freaking, though, unlike the fall, where I just about melted down. The study skills stuff really helped, and I don't need to go there anymore.

Same with the counselor. I got some stuff straightened out. At first, I didn't really know how pissed off I was at Mom, but boy, when I went back and re-read my journal last night, what the counselor had helped me figure out became really clear. Man, I had been pissed about everything she did. I don't feel so pissed off now. I can't believe how much I hated that she made me go to St. Stephen's. That seems like a lifetime ago. Now, I can't really imagine being any place else, and I'm grateful.

That doesn't mean I like the work. Mr. Meader gave me a major break, saying I didn't have to do this journal, and I think you do get used to the work a little, but the bottom line is that it's endless. Since things went smoother for me, I have to start the journal stuff again, so I thought I'd get a jump on it over the break. To be honest, I missed the journal-writing some. It's a good way to clear your head, and I did get a charge out of reading what I'd written. But it was a break not to have to do it for a while.

Winter term was different. For one thing, no exams, so you'd think that would make school easier. But they loaded us up with projects and papers and something called a demonstration, where you have to present your paper to a panel of three teachers in a speech. Then they tear it up, and you have to defend your thesis. I just about crapped my pants. My topic was Voltaire's view of religion, which is something called deism—where God is like a watchmaker who just makes the watch and then leaves it alone to run without interference.

One of the teachers wanted to know whether Voltaire was anti-organized religion or anti-religious faith. Was he just anti-Roman Catholic, or did he mock all faithful people? I hadn't thought about that at all, and tried to B.S. my way through. That didn't work, and the guy said to me, "You haven't thought about this, have you?" I said, "No." He said, "Then just say so. Don't try to fake it." I said, "OK," but I nearly wet my pants in the process. I got a "B" on the thing, though, so that was good.

We did a ton of field trips—the Met in New York, the Barnes Foundation in Philadelphia, the re-done Walters right here in Baltimore, the East Wing of the Smithsonian, and the Holocaust Museum in Washington. We went to Stravinsky's "Rite of Spring" at the Meyerhoff and saw "Tartuffe" at the Lyric. We saw Shakespeare's "Twelfth Night" at Center Stage. We had to write an essay on each one of those trips. The trips were OK, but the writing got old in a hurry because we couldn't just say what happened but had to create a thesis of some sort and then defend it with evidence. I've decided I'm definitely a science-math guy. Like any kind of puzzle or problem just makes sense, but the Humanities stuff has no answers—just a million different ways of looking at it. I just feel like yelling, "OK! So what's the right answer?" But there isn't one.

The best news of the winter is that Mom finished her radiation and has only a few chemo treatments left. She didn't just lose her hair, though. She lost her fingernails and toenails, too. She was sick as a dog all January, and she had no energy. But, she went to work every day, and cooked dinner for us every night. She'd just watch us eat while sipping on a glass of water. It helped that I got my driver's license in January. I'm sixteen now and get back and forth to school by myself. Mom bought a 1998 Volvo station wagon with seventy thousand miles on it. The thing had smelled of dog piss, and nobody would buy it. Some hunter had owned the thing, and his dogs lived in the back. They must have just lifted their legs on everything. Mom got it for $1,500. We ripped out the carpeting in the back, and we scrubbed the thing with this mixture of detergents that Mom concocted. Now the car smells like a hospital. It's pretty much mine to use, which is cool, and it helps Mom out a bunch. I'd never really thought about it before, but getting me back and forth to Baltimore wasted about two and a half hours a day for her. That was on top of her job and taking care of us.

Anyway, they've examined her from top to bottom, and the prognosis is good. She's reacted well to the treatment, and appears to be cancer-free. Of course, it's tough to know because, when it's gotten into lymph nodes, it's sneaky stuff. All of a sudden, it can show up in your liver, or your colon, or your kidneys, or your bones, or your brain, or just about anywhere. You're never out of the woods completely, and they don't say you're cured for more than five years. They check you out every six months or so to see if it comes back. If I'm gonna die from something, I wouldn't choose cancer. I'd rather drown in my waders.

Stephie's been another piece of good news. Maybe it was Mom's cancer. Maybe it's just being eleven. Maybe it was partly me being touchy. Whatever it was, she was a major league pain in the ass last fall and through Christmas. She just needed to be the center of attention all the time. I couldn't get away from her and her whining. If she didn't get her way, she'd throw a fit, and Mom didn't have enough energy to fight her on stuff. Things started to get better this winter, and she's close to being a human again. She actually volunteered to help me get ready for baseball. Yesterday we took a bucket of tennis balls, and she hit them at me with a racket from about twenty feet away. I'd field them and toss them back to her. It's a great way to work on your reactions and footwork. She can hit those tennis balls pretty hard, too.

I'm really psyched for baseball. Mr. Meader gave us a bunch of arm exercises and drills we can do on our own over break. I wish we could practice the way every other school in the league does. We'll be way behind at the start of the season. But the school says "no." They want no school activities of any kind over vacation. Ms. White said, "A vacation from school is exactly that, a complete break from all school activities of any kind. Go do something else. Get some sleep. Be a couch potato. Read a trashy novel. Hang out with friends and family."

Whatever! I've been to a batting cage, and I'm throwing a ball against the garage. Mom got me a great Rawlings glove for my birthday, and I've got it just about where I want it. Mr. Meader says I have a real good shot at making the varsity and maybe even starting at short or second. I've changed my grip on the bat, and I think I'm a little quicker through the strike zone, and I'm sure I'm turning my wrists over faster. Mr. Meader suggested it when I told him I was a little late on fast balls last summer, fouling them off a lot down the first base line. He said he might want to move me back a little more in the batter's box. I've been trying that, too.

Maybe the coolest part of the winter was basketball. Our intramural team was great, but not great enough. We lost in the semis. The "Youglies" took home the trophy and got to play the faculty team, and man, it was no contest. The faculty beat them by about fifteen points. Five of the guys on the teacher's nine-man squad had played in college, and they were awesome.

The varsity squad challenged them, because the faculty was talking major trash. Well, the whole school showed up for a Wednesday afternoon showdown. Ms. White coached the faculty, and they had real referees and everything. Everybody played hard and it was a four-point game at half-time. But then the teachers ran out of gas. The varsity had them in a full court press the whole game, and by the last few minutes, the teachers could barely break out of a walk. We ended up winning by twenty points. It was great. The faculty team had to wait on tables at lunch the next day because that was the bet, and they sang a song to the varsity players that they called, "You are the champions." They better stay teachers because they sure can't sing.

Our basketball varsity team won every game this season. They ruled the tournament in Philadelphia and were ranked number one in the whole country. Our home games were on Friday nights, and they were major social scenes. Everybody wanted to see these guys play. There are a bunch of weird old St. Stephen's traditions, too, and I think they really play with the opponents' heads. Like the opposing team is introduced first, and everybody at St. Stephen's stands and claps for them. Then the St. Stephen's team is introduced. The main lights are dimmed so the place is pretty dark. The fans sit down, and you can hear a pin drop. The place goes completely silent. Each player has his name called and runs onto the court in complete quiet. It's eerie. Some visiting team fans try to break it up by cheering for our players, but find that too weird and give up pretty quickly.

When all the St. Stephen's players go back to the bench, the lights flash on and there's a drum roll. Then the referees are introduced and the place goes wild. The band plays, and everybody beats on trash cans and screams for the refs. First time I was there, it weirded me out, but it's really fun. I don't think the officials are used to being cheered for. Some of them, first-timers, do stuff like take a bow. Then the students stand for the whole game. When the visitors have the ball, we chant "dee-fense, dee-fense" over and over again. It never stops till we get the ball. You can't even hear yourself think.

When we foul someone, the noise gets so incredibly loud you need to cover your ears, right up until the foul shooter from the other team gets the ball. Then the place goes completely silent like someone threw a switch or pressed the mute button. It's so quiet you can hear your heart beat. Sometimes the shooter looks around real quick like,

"What happened," because the quiet is so sudden. Then they'll throw up an air ball or a brick and the place stays silent. Nothing. Nobody in the stands so much as moves. Then, when the game's over and after the players shake hands, the team comes over to the student section, and we all sing verses of the school hymn at the top of our lungs. And I mean everybody sings as loud as they can:

O God our help in ages past,
Our hope for years to come;
Our shelter from the stormy blast,
And our eternal home.

Under the shadow of thy throne,
Thy saints have dwelt secure;
Sufficient is thine arm alone,
And our defense is sure.

Before the hills in order stood,
Or earth received her frame;
From everlasting thou art God,
To endless years the same.

A thousand ages in thy sight,
Are like an evening gone;
Short as the watch that uses the night,
Before the rising sun.

Time like an ever rolling stream,
Bears all her sons away;
They fly forgotten, as a dream
Dies at the opening day.

Jake

Afterward, there's usually a band and food, and everybody hangs out and dances and has a good time. The faculty sticks around, too. They eat and dance and celebrate with us. They say that the same thing happens when we lose, but from this year, I can't speak firsthand about that.

The team went to the White House, hung out with the President, and got their pictures taken. They were in *Sports Illustrated*, too. The article talked about their grade point averages and their SAT scores and their community service as much as about their basketball. After all that, Ms. White gave us a chapel talk about how proud she was of the team, mostly because they hadn't gotten fat heads. She said their humility and dignity said more about their character than did their natural talent. She said that this is what set them apart.

Maybe that's all true, but those guys could flat-out play the game. And I don't think St. Stephen's will see a team like them for a long, long time. If ever.

The only bad thing about the past few months has been the news. I wonder if we'll wind up with a third world war over in the Middle East. These two old men—Arafat and Sharon—have hated each other for so long, they can't imagine not hating each other. They both seem determined to make things as bad as possible. This guy, Arafat, I don't understand at all. It seems to me that he got offered a pretty good deal by Clinton and that Israel had agreed to it, but he just walked away. Now he's got a situation where he's lost everybody's respect. Even his own people don't trust him.

And now this crazy man in Iraq—old Saddam—seems to be gaining prestige. Our allies—the Saudis—are a bunch of thieves, only they're rich thieves with oil. Except for the fact they have oil, I'm having trouble figuring out any good reason for trusting them. I know my knowledge is limited, but I can't help wondering if our entire predicament with terrorists isn't directly linked to our thirst for oil.

This should do it for my first spring term journal entry. Sleep, eat, fish, work on my baseball, and do some chores for Mom—that'll be it for this spring break. That's enough, I think. Then it'll be the big push to June.

IV.

Chapter 18

MARCH 4, 2002—COVER LETTER TO ALL PARENTS
FROM RECTOR MARY WHITE

Dear Karen:

You will find enclosed with this letter our second trimester summary packet. On top is a data sheet, followed by your son's advisor letter, followed by course content descriptions, followed by a grade sheet, and concluded by teacher comments. These materials should give you a thorough sense of your son's work and standing during this academic year's second trimester. If you have any questions, please call your son's advisor first. He will either answer your questions or direct you to someone who can.

The undeniable highlight of winter has been our remarkable varsity basketball team. It is impossible not to be proud of these boys. Hard work, discipline, natural, God-given talent, and superb coaching were obvious and critical ingredients in the extraordinary success these boys enjoyed in becoming the number one ranked high school basketball team in the country. Yet, their humility and humor, grace and selflessness, dignity and sportsmanship, distinguish these boys from most any team I've had the pleasure of watching.

These boys and their coach made us revel vicariously in their achievement. They made us feel good about our school. They made us proud just to be able to cheer for them and call them our own. High school sports, at their best, are the last bastion of undiluted amateurism, where sports are played for the pure, unpolluted joy of participation, where messages of character can still be taught without interference. These boys represented high school athletics at their very finest. We have been lucky to have them with us, and we gratefully thank them for teaching us all enduring lessons from the bully pulpit of the basketball court.

The winter term is always a crowded and busy time at St. Stephen's. Our tenth grade boys took a wide variety of trips, from the opera to the Impressionists, and they wrote dozens of papers. It is fair to say that they are ready for a vacation. We believe that a change of pace in the academic year can be a very good thing, and our winter trimester emphasizes projects, trips, papers, and demonstrations. This is a departure from our more traditional fall and spring curriculum. We hope it develops in the boys an ability to do independent research and work. We also believe that it provides the boys an opportunity to make connections between the classroom and the outside world. Please do call me if you have any comments or suggestions about the winter trimester.

As usual, I conclude on a note of thanks. We are grateful to you for sharing your sons with us, and we are grateful to our faculty and staff who devote their lives to St. Stephen's. Our school is blessed with wonderful people. It is the quality of those people that gives the school its special spirit. Thank you all.

Sincerely,
Mary White
Rector, St. Stephen's Episcopal School

Jake

Karen,

Jake's growth has continued at a wonderful pace. He no longer seems overwhelmed, and his grades, and teacher comments about his performance, indicate significant progress. He seems more at ease, and I often see him in the halls laughing and enjoying the company of teachers and classmates.

Jake has reported to us that you recently received encouraging news from the oncologist. Congratulations! I know your battle is not over, but significant strides in a positive direction deserve celebration.

Please do call me if you have any concerns.

Mary

MR. MEADER'S ADVISOR LETTER, DATED MARCH 2, 2002

Dear Mrs. Collins:

Is it possible that the Jake I know today is the same boy who came to us last August so angry and self-absorbed? Perhaps that is an overly harsh assessment, but it serves to illustrate the progress he has made in just six months. He seems relaxed and engaged. He participates enthusiastically in every area of school life—academics, athletics, and community service.

On the academic front, the comments and grades speak for themselves. The study skills instructor had her last session with Jake two weeks ago. She says he was like a sponge, absorbing what she had to teach quickly and completely. There's no question that his organization, note-taking, and writing skills have improved. He has become much more efficient in separating the wheat from the chaff and emphasizing those academic areas that deserve particular focus. His writing has also improved in terms of mechanics and organization.

In athletics, Jake was an enthusiastic participant in our intramural basketball program. He actually became quite a nice point guard in terms of dribbling and ball handling, but no one will accuse him of being a shooter. His teammates facetiously called him "Brick" at season's end for his less than gentle shooting touch.

The Environmental Club continued to do a great job in and around the Jones Falls. Jake has become a leader in the group and seems sincerely interested in a project to restore trout to the streams in the Jones Falls Watershed.

Jake is a wonderful kid, and you should be very proud of the job he has done. He is delighted with his new driving status, and cheerful about your recent positive prognosis. Congratulations to him and to you.

Sincerely,
George Meader

SECOND TRIMESTER REPORT FOR JAKE PHILLIPS:

Course	Teacher	1st Term Grade	2nd Term Grade
Humanities*	Marks/Smith	D	C
Geometry	Meader	B	A
Physics	Hanson	B	A
French II	Saunders	C	C

*Humanities is reported twice on our official transcript as English and A.P. Modern European History. It is a double period course taught by a teacher from the English Department and a teacher from the History Department along with lecturers from the Art, Music, and Religion Departments.

Sport: Intramural Basketball
Community Service: Environmental Club
Honor Roll for the Second Trimester
(Honor Roll is achieved by earning a "B"
average with no grade below a "C")

TEACHER COMMENTS

Humanities—Kathleen Marks and Jerry Smith

Jake's mechanical problems have all but disappeared. His early inability to create and then support a thesis has also vanished. Jake is not yet a stylish writer, but he has developed a clear, well-organized approach and mastered succinct, efficient sentence structures. Adjectives and adverbs are sparingly used, and he dislikes subordinate clauses. As his confidence grows, however, Jake will learn how to vary his structure and add strong descriptive words to lend power to his nouns and verbs. He deserves strong congratulations on such quick and remarkable improvement.

Jake understands better now the subjective nature of historical and literary scholarship. He is less impatient with tentative conclusions and "either/or" answers. His clear preference is for objective results and what he calls "a right answer," but his sophistication in this area is developing. He is much more willing to consider a variety of views and conclusions.

It has been a pleasure to teach Jake this winter term. (Ask to see his "Voltaire" paper; it's strong work.) He has been a cheerful, consistent class contributor, and he seems to have settled in well to St. Stephen's.

Jake reports that you, too, are doing well. I hope your strength continues to return and that your prognosis remains positive.

Geometry—George Meader

Jake has learned how to "think math." He has evolved from a strong student to an excellent student—one of the best in the class. He seems to enjoy particularly intricate problems in the *fractile* area, and he produces elegant solutions. I have little to offer by way of suggestions for improvement because Jake's winter term work has been genuinely superb. Congratulations!

Physics—Bill Hanson

Jake fixed what was broken! He stands with only a smattering of students in achieving an "A" in this class. His homework and labs continue to be detailed, thorough, and accurate, but his writing and organization have dramatically improved. He states a clear thesis, and he supports it with strong evidence. Jake has evolved from a good student to an excellent student in a very short period of time. I strongly recommend that Jake take both the Physics Advanced Placement Exam and the SAT II Physics Subject Examination this May, and I will talk to him further about those tests.

Congratulations to Jake!

Jake

French II—Helen Saunders

Jake continues to be a diligent, careful French student. He is trying to participate more, but the results are uneven. We have spoken about his difficulty in distinguishing between sounds, and I believe it is fair to say that this is not his strongest natural talent. He seems somewhat amused by his own, often innovative pronunciations, and I am pleased that he has become willing to try without fearing embarrassment. With continued hard work, Jake will improve, but improvement will be incremental and slow. I encourage him not to give up. His progress is steady if unspectacular.

Chapter 19

Baltimore Sun Headlines, March 5-24, 2002

Bush Chides Israelis for Escalation

U.S. Indicts Enron Auditor

Lax Management Blamed at Allfirst

7 U.S. Troops Die in Battle

Hundreds of al-Qaeda, Taliban Killed in Battle

More Afghan, U.S. Troops Join Fighting

Israeli Soldiers Occupy West Bank City, Camps

In Mideast, Deadliest Fighting Yet

2 Attacks, Retaliation in Mideast

Troops Return from Battle

As Israel Buries its Dead, Fears Grow of New Violence

Terrorism Not at End, Bush Warns

Israel Mounts Major Offensive

Gold Medal Day at Towson U. as Leader Installed

Abuse Scandal Costly to Church

Israel Offers Peace Talks

Terror Clouds Peace Effort

Afghan Battle Called Success

Cheney Coaxes Arafat Effort

Senate OKs Campaign Reform Bill

Bomb Derails Mideast Talks

Jake

Good thing I got on top of my journal writing over spring break because the first week back was brutal. I wonder if the teachers suddenly figured out that summer's close, and there's still a ton left to cover. I just handed in the journal entry I'd written three weeks ago, and now the second week is done. I think I'm back in the routine, and the teachers seem to have calmed down a little. At least I feel a little breathing room.

That's good because this is my favorite time of year. How could you not love spring in Baltimore, especially this year? I know the mild winter was supposed to be bad for farmers, and I know the drought is screwing up the water reservoirs. They're letting nothing but a trickle out of Pretty Boy, so the Gunpowder's low. But I can't help myself—I like it. The crocus were up two weeks ago, with the daffodils and forsythias right behind. Everything is blooming like it's April already. We haven't missed a single baseball practice, and we even wore just our long sleeve T-shirts for practice one day. The O's are hot, and they're having a great spring training. They've got a ton of young guys who look hungry. Our infields are smooth. We're in the heart of March madness, and the Terps are looking strong. People say they'll probably screw it up, but I like their chances. We have a big pool going at school. No money is involved, but the winner gets dinner, and all the games he can play in one night for himself and one friend. I'm stoked to win this baby. Go Terps!

Baseball has been great. I've never been to such organized practices. You move right from one thing to the next. There's almost no standing around, and the coaches know what they're doing. I'll probably be at second base this season. They're weak up the middle, but the shortstop from last year has great range even if his arm is a little unpredictable. He's a senior, though, so he deserves the chance. I think maybe second is where I belong anyway. My hands and feet are pretty quick, and I turn a double play OK. I'm not sure I have the arm for a throw from deep in the hole. The shortstop has got to really let that sucker go, and I'd have to get too much air under the ball to beat a speedy runner to first.

Anyway, everybody's loving being out there. We had a practice game, and everybody got a chance to play. I went 2 for 3—two line drives up the middle and then a squirrelly little pop that the catcher fielded. I didn't keep my head down on that one. Our team pretty much cruised. Their pitchers were struggling. Life is good on the baseball diamond. The crummy articles in the newspapers, all the work for school, Mom's cancer—they all disappear for that little piece of time that I'm completely focused on hitting and fielding, running and throwing. As different from baseball as fishing is, it does the same thing. It's a shelter when the sky is raining down garbage.

And that's pretty much what's happening in the world. What a contrast to spring time in Maryland, where there's new life popping up all over the place! There's death everywhere else. The fighting in Afghanistan is getting our guys killed now. The Israelis and the Palestinians are butchering each other as fast as they can. We're scared of being butchered right here at home. There's all sorts of crap about businessmen cheating, and even a giant business like Enron keels over and collapses with the help of accountants who are sup- posed to tell the truth about financial stuff. To top that off, you've got priests, PRIESTS!, who have been molesting children, and, not just the Catholic Church, but our whole legal system has been covering it up. However awful it is, though, it all seems far away. I read about it, and it seems like it's all in another world.

We've been talking about this stuff in class a lot, which helps make it more real. The teachers keep this stuff in front of us, maybe even too much. Ms. Marks has pointed out some interesting parallels to late 15th and early 16th century Europe, when the Reformation happened. There was corruption and death and war everywhere then, too, but big time changes happened in society. Things aren't completely the same now, of course, but it's interesting to see that human beings have been pretty shitty to each other forever. Boy, that Holocaust Museum in Washington will show you that. It just about made me sick to my stomach. Those baby shoes were too much! If you're born at the wrong time, you can suffer your whole life, with no relief in sight. A guy in class said that life is like Russian Roulette, with three of the six cylinders loaded. He's a cynic, but I get his point.

I got some disappointing news last Saturday morning. Joel and I had given our water temperature and habitat data to a fisheries management guy a month ago, then we met with him to hear if trout could go into any part of the Jones Falls below Lake Roland. I pretty much knew what was coming because most of the stream is a culvert. Some of it is underground, and lots of it is under the highway. I did have some hope for the area just below the Lake Roland dam because the water gets aerated and cooled from falling about twenty feet, and there's a section after the waterfall that has some nice riffles, some good deep holding pools, and a lot of shade. It looks trouty to me, and the winter temperature readings were hopeful. I turned over some rocks and found some larva, too. Encouraging!

But the guy said no. He said the stretch of stream that could sustain trout is too short. There would be no holdovers. They'd all be dead by August. Even if you put them in as put-and-take fish, expecting them to be caught before August, it wouldn't be worth it because they'd be stressed and unhealthy. I'm pretty bummed. I like the idea of catching trout inside city limits. There are fish in the Jones Falls, but they're all bottom feeders. Even in the culvert, life manages to hold on—frogs and minnows and stuff. I guess the herons I see down there under the bridges aren't as dumb as they look. It is truly amazing how life hangs on even in the most screwed-up environment, where we've done everything we can to make the place disgusting and lifeless. Life seems to adapt and get used to sterile, even toxic, surroundings. That stinking, shallow culvert under the bridges must have been a beautiful country stream a century ago. I'd compare life for a heron or a frog there now to life on the Gaza Strip for Palestinians. It stinks, but it's all you've got, so you just hang on. But you might get pissy from all the poison and act like a jerk. Like that heron that got caught in the trap. It couldn't help itself, but, boy, it was sure going to smack the hell out of anyone else who tried to help it.

On the brighter side of things, Stephie, Mom, and I went out on the Gunpowder earlier this evening. Stephie doesn't fish, but she likes to ride her bike on the path, the way Hank and I used to when we were her age. Her attention runs out after about an hour, so our time in the water is short. That's OK since I have plenty of homework. Mom caught a humongous brown under the bank in only about two feet of water. It must have been cruising upstream looking for minnows. She slapped a big bead-head wooly booger about three quarters upstream and let it bounce along the bottom past her and under the bank. She gave it a few twitches just before retrieving it for another short roll cast, and "boom," she thinks it's snagged. I'm close by trying to untangle a mess I've made, and I hear her say "shit!" under her breath, which is not Mom's normal vocabulary. And then she says real loud, "Holy moly, beans and guacamole!"

Where does she come up with such lame sayings? It must be the Texas part of her that sneaks out. When I say something stupid, she says, "That dog won't hunt," or when she watched Roger Clemens pitch on TV, she said, "Why, that boy could throw a ripe strawberry through a closed barn door." She's lived on the east coast a long time, but I guess she just can't shake that Texas stuff. She said, "Why, Stephie, you're smarter then a tree full of owls," when her report card came last June. She hasn't said anything queer like that for a long time. It only happens when she's happy.

So I know when I hear the "beans and guacomole" line that it's a good fish she's got, and she's not thinking about anything else. She's using a four-weight line and a light leader, so it takes her a while to land that fat momma. She can't just horse him in. But she does a good job. The whole time she's singing a song she hasn't sung, at least in my hearing, for about a year. She used to hum it or sing it damn near all the time when things were going well, or when she was preoccupied with something else. She claimed it just came out of her without her even knowing it—"The Yellow Rose of Texas"—or something like that. She's not wearing a hat or a bandana, and her head is sort of fuzzy, like a baby's head. She said, "to hell with covering up this nobby head of mine," some time ago. It's good to see her making a comeback.

We all looked at the fish she snagged. I'd say it was close to twenty inches. We could have kept it because we weren't in catch and release water. We were down just a couple hundred yards east of York Road. But Mom said, "No, this one's just too pretty to take out of the river. She needs to live long and well. We'll catch her and her children again."

That's right, I think.

Chapter 20

Baltimore Sun Headlines, April 2, 2002

Champions, Gritty Terps Claim 1st NCAA Title

School Girl, 11, Killed Crossing Road

Speeding Teen Crests Hill and Ignores School Bus with Flashing Lights
Girl's Body Recovered from Gunpowder River—
Thrown over Guard Rail to Water Below

HEREFORD—Stephanie Phillips, age 11, was pronounced dead at Greater Baltimore Medical Center having been struck by a car while crossing Little Falls Road from her school bus yesterday. Her body was recovered from the water on the Gunpowder River below the Little Falls Bridge, where it was thrown by the impact of the Ford Explorer driven by Shawn Gorman, 18, of Hereford.

School Bus number 362, driven by Enis Schafner, followed its prescribed route from Hereford Middle School through Hereford, along Mt. Carmel Road and north on Little Falls Road before stopping in its approved location just after crossing the Little Falls Bridge.

"I turned on the flashing red lights, just like I always do, when we started over the bridge," said Mrs. Schafner, a fifteen-year veteran school bus driver, "and the stop sign flipped out just like always. I don't let the children out unless cars have stopped or the way is clear. That SUV just came from nowhere, and it never slowed down. I yelled out at Stephie to stop just as she crossed in front of the bus, but she did-n't hear me."

Gorman, the SUV driver, and his four passengers, all seventeen-year-old minors, are seniors at Hereford High School. According to one of the passengers, who asked to remain anonymous, "we were just cruising and laughing and singing with the radio like any day after school, and then there was this bang and Shawn started screaming, 'Oh my God, oh my God,' and we, like, didn't even know what had happened until afterward."

Gorman was taken into custody by the Hereford Sheriff's Office and, after questioning, was released into the custody of his parents, Malcolm and Hester Gorman. He had no comment about the acci-dent, but a family spokesperson, Harold Carol, said, "Shawn is deeply saddened by the death of the little girl and regrets this terrible and tragic accident." Mr. Carol refused to comment further on any aspect of the event, saying only, "I am sure you will appreciate the necessity of Shawn's silence on this matter, but I do know he and his family offer heartfelt condolences to the family of Stephanie Phillips."

Stephanie Phillips is survived by her mother, Karen Collins, and her brother, Jake Phillips. Neither was available for comment.

The Hereford Sherriff's Department is investigating the accident and will have no comment until the investigation is concluded, its spokesperson says.

Chapter 21

APRIL 1, 2002 AT 10:00 PM—MEMORANDUM TO FACULTY
AND STAFF FROM RECTOR MARY WHITE IN BOTH E-MAIL
AND HARD COPY

I wanted you to have this information before the start of the school day this Wednesday morning.

It is with great sadness that I inform you of a family and personal tragedy that has befallen a member of our school community. Jake Phillips, a new tenth grader whom we all have come to know with affection as a boy of considerable talent and genuine warmth, suffered the loss of his sister, Stephie, earlier this afternoon.

Stephie, who was eleven, was struck by a car and killed after she got off her school bus. There is simply no gentle way to report this horrible fact.

Jake is staying at school in the third floor dorm. As I write to you, I am unsure whether he will choose to participate in the school routine. He will be visiting with our counselor and chaplain tomorrow morning (today, as you read this on Wednesday morning), and so will not be in morning classes.

I intend to speak to the students about this tragedy in morning chapel, and I will let you know more about this situation as information comes to me.

Please join me in prayer for Jake and his mother, Karen. It will take the full support of our entire community to help this little family confront and deal with this terrible ordeal. Jake and Karen have difficult times ahead of them, and it is our duty to help them along that uncertain path.

WEDNESDAY, APRIL 2, 2002—CHAPEL TALK, DELIVERED BY RECTOR MARY WHITE

It is with deep sadness that I speak to you today. A member of our school community is in terrible pain, and we suffer with him. Let me tell you what I know.

Jake Phillips' little sister, Stephie, who was eleven years old, was killed yesterday. She had just gotten off her school bus and was crossing the road when an oncoming car struck her.

Jake learned of this accident yesterday afternoon during sports period. As you can imagine, Jake is deeply affected. Some of you already know that Jake stayed here at school last night. His mother needed to attend to some issues surrounding this tragedy. A sudden shock like this can cause us to react in unpredictable ways. Sometimes we deny that a tragedy has happened. Sometimes we become numb. Sometimes we become overly emotional. Sometimes we become angry. And sometimes, at different moments, we combine all these ways of reacting.

Jake will be grieving in his own way. We are his community, his source of strength. We have a duty to grieve with him, to help him in any way we can. Individuals who suffer terrible tragedy can best deal with their grief in the context of a group of people who love and care about them.

What can you do to help? It depends, of course, on how close you are personally to Jake. The closer you are, and the better you know him, the more you can be of help. If you are unsure what to do, speak to your advisor, the chaplain, the counselor, me, or any other faculty member with whom you feel comfortable. Here are some general guidelines: Be kind and understanding. Treat Jake as you would want to be treated under the same circumstances. Understand that he might react awkwardly or harshly to anything you might say or do. If you feel moved to do so, write Jake a note expressing your sadness and support. His address is in the student directory.

You may be self-conscious in the presence of Jake's sadness, but please do not avoid him or look the other way. Include him in your conversations and activities as you always would. Do not feel that he needs or wants to be the center of attention. He may want to sit quietly in a group and listen to conversation. Feel free to say to him something simple like, "Jake, I'm sorry." Don't feel that you have to be profound. Simple gestures and short statements of support are eloquent. He needs to know that we care, and simple things can accomplish that.

Some of us have suffered our own tragedies, and the personal tragedy of another can bring to the surface deep feelings of grief that we thought we had put behind us. That is an entirely understandable reaction. It stems from empathy. But please don't deal with those feelings alone. Talk to your advisor if you are feeling particularly low. Talk to the chaplain or the counselor. Don't suffer by yourself. Whatever differences we may have on the surface of things, we are all, first and foremost, human beings. We suffer the same fears and pains. We and those whom we love all have the same terminal illness—we are all mortals. That binds us together in our shared humanity. It gives us empathy. We are capable of feeling and understanding one another's deepest sadness. This is what makes us human. It is the pain of the human soul.

Jake

Let us then share Jake's grief. Let us support him individually and collectively in the best ways we know how. I know you boys well, and this is when you are at your best. Thank you, and I am sorry for bringing you such sad news.

APRIL 2, 2002—HANDWRITTEN LETTER
FROM MARY WHITE TO JAKE

Dear Jake:

No words are adequate to describe the sadness you must be feeling right now. Please know that my thoughts and prayers are with you. It is hard to find comfort in much of anything after such a grievous loss as the death of a sister, but I, and all of us at St. Stephen's, yearn to be a refuge and a comfort to you should you need us. We are here and at your service. We care deeply about you and your mother and offer you our condolences and our hearts.

I will be presumptuous here and offer you one small thought for your consideration. Be a source of strength for your mother if you can summon up the courage. There is nothing more devastating for a parent than the death of a child. It is a tragedy from which parents never fully recover. Your mother will need your help, your strength, and, above all else, your love. However acute your grief is, your mother suffers more acutely. And, as you know from your time at St. Stephen's, one way to lighten one's own burden is to take on the burden of another.

Our love is with you.

Sincerely,
Mary White
Rector, St. Stephen's Episcopal School

April 2, 2002—Handwritten Letter
from George Meader to Jake

Dear Jake:

Please excuse my inability to control my emotions when you are the one who is suffering the most heart-breaking unhappiness. I admit to selfishly thinking of my own children, how precious they are to me. I know that you and Stephie were close. I met her only twice, but she was a bright-eyed, energetic sprite of a girl. You are, I know, missing her terribly.

I am sorry beyond my ability to express it. There is just nothing good or fair or just about the death of a young child. It leaves you helpless. All you can do is remember the good. Remember the wonderful times you enjoyed with Stephie. You will always have those times. They are yours and cannot be taken away from you. Also, remember me and your many other friends here at St. Stephen's. We care about you. We grieve with you. You are not alone.

Please call on me if there is any way I can be of help.

Sincerely,
George Meader

Jake

The funeral service for Stephanie Phillips, the sister of Jake Phillips, will be at 10:30 am on Wednesday, April 10th, 2002 at the St. George's Church. Please inform your advisor during today's advisory meeting if you would like to attend the service. Bus transportation from St. Stephen's will be provided, as will transportation back to school after the service. You will be excused from class should you choose to attend.

Chapter 22

JOURNAL ENTRY: MAY 30, 2002

Who could have written during the last two months? I couldn't, and I wouldn't if I could have. We gathered at school this morning, though, and watched the Ground Zero Ceremony. I started crying when they rang the silver bell, not sobbing or anything, but just tears like a fountain and unable to speak. All those families, and all their dead brothers and sisters and mothers and fathers and sons and daughters. When they played taps, I thought I would throw up, it hurt so much. Nobody said anything to me. One guy I hardly know, Pete Zendt, was sitting next to me. He just put his arm across my shoulders, and we just kept watching.

This is the first time I've really fallen apart. On April 1st, it was as if someone had flipped a switch and turned off every emotion besides anger and a sense of lonely emptiness. It's not lost on me that she was killed on April Fool's Day, like some big cosmic joke. Angry, numb, angry, numb. It's been back and forth. Despair too. Complete despair. I feel like writing now. I'm not completely sure why. It's been a bad couple of months. Very bad. And things probably won't get better for awhile.

Probably the reason I want to write is I want to remember how I

Jake

feel. Like looking back over my journal from the fall, I didn't remember resenting Mom for sending me to St. Stephen's. Things had changed over only six months, and I'd already forgotten how I felt at the start. I want to remember what has happened, what I did, how I felt. Even now, April 1st seems like a long time ago. So much has happened so fast. Sometimes I almost feel as though this has all happened in somebody else's life, that I can just close my eyes, open them a moment later, and the whole deal will have been a dream. No such luck.

⁂

I was on my way out to the baseball diamond when Mr. Meader called out to me. "Hey, Jake," he said, "Ms. White wants to see you up in her office."

He looked a little funny. His expression was off, sort of strained. "Why?"

"Go find out. Hustle up now. Not good to keep the rector waiting."

I remember being irritated. I didn't want to miss that time before practice when we do long toss or play pepper or just screw around. So I ran. I wasn't worried because I hadn't been doing anything wrong. I was a bit curious, though. I remember looking over my shoulder at Coach Meader. He was just standing there watching me, and his shoulders were sort of slumped. "What's wrong with him?" I wondered. I didn't have a clue.

I got to the office carrying my cleats, just in my socks, and the secretary said to me, "Go right in." So I did. Ms. White was behind her desk and she stood up. "Hello, Jake, take a seat on the couch. I'll be right with you." She went out of the office for about five minutes. I couldn't see exactly what she was doing from where I was sitting, but the wait was just about killing me. I was squirming around thinking, "Damn, damn, damn, the best part of the day and I'm missing it."

Then she walked back in the office, and Coach Meader was behind her. He closes the office door, and he's carrying his cleats, just wearing his socks, looking like a sad little fat kid who got called into the principal's office. His face is saggy like a hound dog's, and he won't look me in the eye. He puts his cleats on the floor, his hat on the table, and sits next to me on the couch, way forward on it, only on the front three inches or something, and he's real close to me, violating my personal space, if you know what I mean, but he still won't look at my face. Something's up, and it's not good. Finally, I'm getting worried.

Ms. White sits in one of the chairs across the table from the couch, and she looks at me for what seems like a long time. She sighs, looks away like she's thinking hard, and then she looks back at me. Her eyes are wet. She's not crying. She's under control, but her eyes have a liquid look to them and she starts to talk in a quiet, sad way that gives me goose bumps.

"Jake, I have terrible news that you need to hear, and there is no gentle or kind way to tell you. Your mother asked me to speak with you and tell you this news, which she would ordinarily tell you herself. For reasons that you will come to understand, she is unable to tell you now, and has asked me, so that you do not get the information through another source."

To say I was freaked out at this point is an understatement, but I still didn't have a clue.

"About an hour ago, your sister, Stephie, got off her school bus in the usual spot. She began to cross the road just as she always does, when a car coming in the other direction at a high speed struck and killed her."

"What?" I said. "What?" And Ms. White said nothing. She just looked at me with this sad, helpless face.

"No!" I remember shouting, and I stood up fast and banged the table and knocked off this little sand box with a little miniature rake and pebbles. It was on the table. Now it was nothing but a pile of sand on the rug.

Mr. Meader stood up with me, and I said, "no" again, but I know now. Somewhere I know and the "no" I say, again, over and over, is empty, meaningless. But I have no words, and I look at her face and then his face. She's looking at me. He's looking at his feet, but he suddenly hugs me, a big bear hug that almost squeezes the breath right out of me. My arms are pinned at my sides, and he's shaking. I don't have feelings. I can't sort things out. Things crowd into my head too fast for my thoughts to stick. They all slide out of my mind. It's like a moving collage where you're never allowed to look at a picture long enough to understand it. You know what the pictures are, but you don't know what they mean.

But Mr. Meader has feelings, and he's hugging me and shaking, and I know he's crying. After a little while, he lets me go, and we both sit down. Ms. White hands him something to wipe his nose. I don't know where those tissues came from. They just appeared like magic. And, still, I've got nothing to say. I have this terrible sick feeling. It's not nausea—not like I'm going to puke. It's more like something broke, like a chain coming off a bicycle and the pedals don't work, or the tip of your rod snapping when you close it in the car door. It's not like there's much to say when any of that happens. You just swear, and it is what it is. "Fuck!" you might scream. But this is past that. This is way past "fuck." There just isn't a word worth saying.

But then I want details, and I make Ms. White tell me again, and

I ask questions, but she doesn't know any more than what she has just said. We sit silently for a moment and then I ask, "What now? What happens now?"

"Mr. Meader and I are going to go with you to the hospital, GBMC, where your mom is and where Stephie's body is . . ."

"Stephie's body." I missed the rest of what she said. Stephie's body, not Stephie, is sitting at the hospital. I couldn't get my arms around that idea. Her body, not her. Ms. White must have seen I wasn't listening. When I zoned back in, I said, "Sorry."

"It's OK, Jake," she said. "Your mom is badly shaken by this, as you can imagine. She's had to be treated for shock, and she is resting comfortably now, from what we are told. But they had to give her a sedative to calm her. We should go see her. She wants to see you."

Ms. White drove us out of the city, with me in the front seat, and Mr. Meader in the back. I don't think we said more than two words the whole way. At the hospital, Ms. White seemed to know what she was doing. A young guy in a white coat—a resident I think is what he called himself—met us in the lobby. He turns out to be a St. Stephen's graduate from late in the 1980s. He hugs Ms. White, shakes Mr. Meader's hand, and then shakes mine, too, and says, "I'm sorry for your loss."

"Thanks," I mumble.

"My loss" . . . How odd, I'm thinking to myself. "My loss." Like when you lose one slipper and the other one's worthless. Like when you lose a fly because your cast sucked and the thing is snagged too high in a tree branch for you to get it. "I've lost a goddam sister!" I feel like shouting. Not a slipper! Not a fly! It's more like a body part walked off unexpectedly. You try to shake hands, but you don't have hands. Surprise! Look, Mom, no hands!

That's how my head was working. Thoughts would pile on top of other thoughts in no logical order until they were just a heap in some corner of my brain like garbage in an alley. And then I'd just leave them there, and start another pile of thoughts in another alley of my brain. And some of those piles made sense, not by themselves, and not as a group. They were just random.

"Your mother," this white coat was talking to me as the four of us are walking down the hall, "wants to see you very much, but she's in a fragile condition. Her emotions are near the surface. She became exercised and agitated when she viewed your sister's body, and then the strain seemed to be too much. She collapsed, and we've admitted her to the hospital for observation. She is sedated heavily, so don't be surprised or concerned if her speech is slow and a little funny or if she has trouble getting her thoughts together. You also need to know she's in restraints. We were worried that she might hurt herself, because she'd become hard to control."

"Oh," I said.

We got on an elevator and got off on some floor; I don't know which one. We walk down one hall, then another, and suddenly we're in Mom's room. It's dark, and she looks tiny under this sheet that's over her. I walk over to her bed and say, "Hi, Mom."

She opens her eyes when she hears my voice, and she looks at me for about two seconds, and then she tries to raise her arms, but she can't. "Oh, Jake," she says. "Oh, Jake, come here . . ."

She's confused about why she can't raise her arms, and as I lean over her to give her a hug, she's starting to panic, "Why can't I hug my son? Why can't I hug my son?" she kind of gurgles out in a halting, thick voice.

"Undo her," I say, and the resident is already working on one of her wrists. I undo the other. She puts her arms around my neck and pulls me tight down toward her. She's strong for such a skinny little person, and she clings to me like I'm the only thing keeping her from falling off a bridge. And then she's sobbing, her whole body shaking, and she says over and over, "Poor Stephie, poor poor Stephie . . ."

And that was pretty much the whole visit. It became pretty obvious she needed to stay right where she was. Her mind wandered, and she fell asleep in mid-sentence. Seeing Mom fighting cancer was different. She might have been exhausted, but for the most part she still had an edge to her. Underneath all that sickness and exhaustion, Mom was still in there. There wasn't much to recognize about the little white-skinned, fuzzy-headed person under the sheet in that dark room. We left and drove back to school.

I stayed at school, in the dorm on the third floor, the next week. There was no use going home, and Ms. White said I should stay. I didn't know it at first, but from seeing Mr. Meader at breakfast the next morning, I figured out he was staying at school, too. He'd cleared off that crowded couch of his and was sleeping right there in his office, keeping an eye on me. Ms. White was there for breakfast, too, and she had dropped by the dorm that night at about ten to see how I was doing. At first, the other kids didn't know how to act around me. They seemed to be curious about how I was doing. They were sympathetic and sad. They'd look at me and then look away. But they didn't have words for it.

Me either. There were no words, and there weren't even feelings during that week at school while Mom was trying to pull herself together. Except I started being pissed off. Angry at that asshole driving the car. Angry at Mom for falling apart. Angry at Stephie for I don't know what. And then guilty for being angry at Stephie, so then I'd be angry at myself. Then I'd get angry—angry at life in general. I got angry at a newspaper article that just added more facts. The driver had been going over 50 miles per hour, and Stephie wasn't killed from the impact. She drowned in the Gunpowder River. Drowned!

I had trouble sleeping at night, so I'd fall asleep in class. I just kept going to my regular appointments, kept going to practice. I only missed morning classes on that first day, Wednesday. I was talking to the counselor, then to the chaplain. I didn't have much to say, and they seemed to respect that. I did regular school stuff, which kept me busy even if I was really off someplace, inside my own head.

Mr. Meader went with me to the hospital on Saturday to pick up Mom. She met us in the lobby sitting in a wheelchair. They made her do that. She couldn't remember where she'd parked the car. We finally found it parked in the emergency lot. I drove her home. A friend from St. George's Church, Mrs. Pine, was at home. She had cleaned the place. On the dining room table was a ton of mail. There were flowers everywhere: in the living room, in the kitchen, in the front hall, everywhere. The refrigerator was jammed with food. Somebody had mowed the lawn. Somebody had driven the Volvo home from school. I'd forgotten about it completely.

Mom went upstairs to lie down. She said hello and thanks to Mrs. Pine. It was as if the trip home had exhausted her. She walked up the stairs slowly, leaning on the handrail. I started reading the mail that was in a pile and addressed to me. It took me all afternoon. Every teacher in school must have written me. Members of the kitchen staff wrote. Guys from the grounds crew, too. My friends had written, but so had students who I barely knew.

I liked reading the letters. I don't know why, since most of them were forced and awkward. Again, the words just weren't there for people. But it wasn't the words that mattered so much. I guess it was just the writing that mattered, not what was said. Ms. White had written a letter, too. It was classic Ms. White. She was sad and all that, like everybody else, but she also wanted me to take care of Mom. She said that as awful as life seemed for me personally, it was much worse for Mom. "There's just nothing more devastating for a parent than the death of a child. It's a tragedy from which parents never fully recover. She'll need your help, your strength, and above all else your love." That made me think. It made me angry, too, like everything else was making me angry. My sister's dead, and she's giving me advice. I don't need her advice, I remember thinking; I need Stephie back.

Mrs. Pine came into the dining room, where I was reading at about 6:00. "There's a chicken casserole in the oven and a salad in the fridge. I'm going home now. Are you alright?"

I was and said so. She left saying that another lady from church would be over in the morning. Reverend Gordon, the minister at St. George's, would visit around lunch, after church services, but he would call first to see if that was convenient. All of this and a bunch of phone messages were on a pad by the phone for Mom to look at when she was ready.

Mom came down at about 6:30. We ate the casserole and the salad. They were good. We didn't say much. She looked up at me once and said, "Are you OK, Jake? How are you holding up?"

"Good," I said. "I'm good, Mom. Don't worry about me."

We were quiet again for a few mouthfuls, and I said, "How are you doing? Are you OK?"

She chewed on a mouthful of casserole for about half a minute before answering. "Not so good, honey. I'm just barely hanging on. But it'll get better. It can't get worse . . ."

Her voice just trailed off. We sat there in the quiet. She got up from the table and said she was going to bed. She hadn't read any mail, and she'd only eaten about half of what was on her plate. I told her about what Mrs. Pine had said and about the phone messages, but she didn't say anything. She just started up the stairs.

⬥

That was the worst night for me. I cleaned up and then tried to watch some TV. I couldn't stand anything that was on. Even the Orioles game against the Mariners was boring. World Cup Soccer was on ESPN, but that was no good. On CNN and Fox News, they're all talking about India versus Pakistan, or how our FBI should have known about September 11th. Over and over again the experts repeat themselves.

So after I turned the tube off, I wandered around the house and wound up in Stephie's room. I lay on her bed and stared at the ceiling. I sat at her desk and looked in her drawers. I opened her bureau and held up one of her T-shirts and smelled it. I went to her closet and smelled her pajamas that were hung up on a hook. I sat on the floor with her big stuffed bear. All this time I have this feeling that I have no feeling, that someone else is walking around her room, or maybe that this is all made up—a long bad dream. I'll wake up any second.

I went outside and walked around the house. The stars were out but not clear because the moon was big and bright. The tree frogs and crickets and bugs were kicking up their usual noise. I stood still and listened, and I got this urge to go to the river, to go to the Gunpowder and see where Stephie got thrown off the bridge. I've been over that spot a hundred times. I've fished the spot where she drowned. Drowned!

I thought about the two dead guys. They'd also drowned—one of them in my Gunpowder. An important guy whose waders filled up. The other in a polluted, pathetic little urban creek. Nobody knew him, and nobody cared. To me, they were the same. But now Stephie was as dead as those dead guys, drowned in my river, my water, breathing it into her lungs, swallowing it into her stomach until she's more river than my sister. "She sleeps with the fishes." I remembered that gangster line from some movie, my mind still going off to places that I wasn't in charge of. Random places that made no sense. But I needed to go to that river. Not in the dark, though.

So I went up to my room and lay on my bed waiting for light. Sometime around 2 a.m., I heard Mom walk past my bedroom. She opened Stephie's bedroom door. I heard some shuffling around for awhile, and then silence. After a while, I heard this sound, something like the sound some dogs make when a siren goes past. It was a half-moan, half-howl. It was lower than that, though, like something that would scare you half to death if you heard it in the woods at night. I know it was Mom. She was in there the way I had been, trying to feel Stephie's life, trying to make her alive, trying to grab hold of something that you know you can't hold. And she was wishing she could trade places, wishing something could happen to erase April 1st, April Fool's Day. After a while, she stopped. Stephie's door opened and closed. Footsteps went past my door. Mom's bedroom door closed. There was silence, except those country night noises that let you know that the woods are alive and the fields are full, and that nothing has changed at all out there, however much it has changed inside you.

Jake

The second there's enough light to see my hand in front of my face, I'm up. I left Mom a note saying I'd gone for a bike ride, and I grabbed my fishing stuff from the garage, shoved it in my backpack, and headed for the river. It's just a little drift down the hill to the Little Falls bridge, and the air was early morning cool. The bugs, who like to swarm on the edges of light and dark, were still asleep or doing whatever it is bugs do. I stowed my bike in the woods, assembled my rod, and climbed into my waders. I tied a #16 blue-winged olive on my tippet and walked up on the bridge. It was getting lighter, and I could see down into the black water rolling under my feet. "There's the pool where Stephie drowned," I thought to myself, but I wasn't thinking clearly as usual. I was real tired, almost too tired to move, so I just stared down into that water that drowned my sister. The sun was up by the time I got myself together enough to walk off the bridge and down to the pool, and then I just stood there again like a cow.

And then I acted in ways that probably seem stupid. It's embarrassing now, but I want to remember the things I did. I don't want to forget, even if they were stupid and senseless.

I got down on my hands and knees on the edge of the pool where I think Stephie must've drowned, and I stared into it. Then I lay down on my stomach and put my face in the water. I opened my eyes in the water and stared at nothing, and then I exhaled through my nose and mouth, feeling the bubbles rise around my ears. Then I breathed in.

It was like a stab in the chest with a sharp knife, and I yanked my head out of the water without even knowing I was doing it. I coughed and gagged and almost threw up before I could get any air at all. The first few breaths hurt, but then my lungs started to work better. I stood up but was so dizzy I had to sit down and then lie down. I listened to the roar of the Gunpowder, and I watched the leaves above me waving in the wind. My head was almost completely empty for a while and that felt good.

But then the same angry feeling crept back into me. I got up and walked upstream, past some excellent pools. I saw some rises behind a boulder, but I wasn't there to fish. My legs took me all the way to the pool where they found the rich dead guy. I didn't stop. I just stripped off my wader belt and walked part-way into that pool, hip-deep. Then I inched forward until the water was right at the top of the waders. Some came over the top and I could feel the cold ooze down my belly. I could feel it chill my crotch, creep down my legs, and then form in puddles around my feet as my socks got soaked.

I had the same kind of random thought I'd been having. I thought about that heron with its legs in a trap, how it broke that guy's collarbone when he was trying to help it, and then how a bunch of people grabbed that stupid bird and fixed it. I thought about baseball, about turning my wrists over, about standing farther back in the box. I thought about the Judge and how he loved Socrates. I thought about Ms. White and her talks—not about anything she said really—but just about her talking: From the pulpit, in her office, at the pep rally, in the dining hall. I thought about Mom in her hospital bed, in Stephie's room moaning all alone in the dark. These thoughts weren't in a row. They didn't come one by one but all at once and in no order, but I can remember them even now.

I'd had enough of the cold water in my waders, and I backed slowly out of the pool and onto the bank. I walked back to my bike and I rode home. It was 8:15 and Mom wasn't yet in sight. I made breakfast: Bacon, scrambled eggs, English muffins with marmalade, coffee, and O.J. I put it on a tray and went upstairs to Mom's room. I went in, and she was awake.

"Hi, honey," she said.

"Breakfast, Mom. Time to eat."

Jake

She did.

❦

Because Mom had been in the hospital all last week, there were no plans for a funeral or anything at all. That's what Reverend Gordon had come to see us about. A lady from the church, Mrs. Horton, had already come and gone. The minister stayed for about two hours. I didn't have much to say and just listened. The service would be Wednesday morning at 10:30. Friends would be welcome back at our house afterwards, and the ladies from the church wanted to take care of refreshments, which was fine with Mom. I called Ms. White at her house and told her.

I didn't go to school on Monday or Tuesday. I called Mr. Meader and told him I needed to hang out with Mom. Every night she went into Stephie's room, and every night I heard that moan, like pain that went from nerve endings to sound waves.

We got to the church early and went straight to the parish house, where there was a little living room area where we could sit quietly. The minister came in and spoke to us for a moment. Ms. White came in, too. Mom had wanted her to say a few words, so she must have showed up early to get with the minister for details and what not. Then this smiling lady came in. I'd seen her around the church a lot, but I didn't know her name. She gave Mom a big hug and me a big kiss that was wet and smelled like cotton candy. Then she said, and I'll never forget it, "Jesus called her home. The Lord wanted your sweet child. God shows his love in mysterious ways." She was smiling with her whole face. I didn't cave in her face with my fist, but I came close. Mom's expression went from blank to what she'd look like if she'd tasted something bad. After the lady left, Mom looked at me and said very gently, "God isn't in the child-killing business, Jake. He didn't want Stephie dead."

And then, who should push the door open and stick his head in but a taller version of . . . Hank!

"Can I come in?" he said.

"Yeah," I yelled, and I walked over and gave him a big hug. He hugged hard back. Then he looked over at Mom with a real shy look like he didn't know how to act. The two of them hadn't seen too many things the same way when he lived with us.

Mom said, "Hello, Hank, bring your tall self over here and give your old evil stepmother a hug."

He was crying before he even reached her. He said over and over, "I'm so sorry. I'm so sorry . . ." They hugged for a long time, and I hadn't even noticed at first that our old seventh grade English teacher, Mr. Finks, had slipped quietly into the room behind Hank. I turned toward him, and he stepped forward and shook my hand. Same smudged glasses. Same uneven moustache. He said, "I hope you're holding up alright, Jake. I brought Hank over. I hope you don't mind my intrusion."

"No, Mr. Finks, no. I'm glad to see you and real glad to see Hank."

I introduced Mom to Mr. Finks. She remembered him. He excused himself, but I asked Hank to stay. He was a mess, I'll tell you. He'd been close to Stephie, probably closer than me in some ways. He could play with her for hours and never get bored. She'd be Barbie and he'd be Ken, and Barbie would just kick the hell out of Ken in some game, but old Ken (a.k.a. Hank) would come back for more. I had trouble dragging information out of him because he was so emotional. "I just heard on Saturday," he said, shaking his head. "It's so wrong, It's so unfair."

Jake

Life in Virginia has been OK for him. He says Norfolk isn't worse than any other place. He claims he got lucky with a good English teacher in ninth grade last year. "A female version of Finks," he said. "Imagine that!" She got him involved in some young writer's program, and he's all caught up in the school newspaper and the poetry club and the literary magazine. He says every other part of school sucks. The teacher's don't know you from any other of the twenty-eight kids in the class, and they seem more interested in the end of class than the inside of class. He claims he's learned to tolerate bullshit a little better, but says he's not yet in my league. I can't imagine him being able to put up with too much garbage without doing something crazy.

His mother is still a doper and still married to that guy. Hank says he just steers clear of them as much as he can. He stays in touch with old Finks, and he reads books that Finks sends him. They talk by phone once a week, and Finks has him keeping a journal the way we do at St. Stephen's. And Hank's playing baseball again. He's a pitcher, starting for the varsity, and playing some right field or first base when he's not on the mound.

"What happened to short?" I asked.

"My legs got tangled up too much. Big feet—size twelves."

But I sort of dragged out of him the fact that he's batting close to .400 and he's 6-3 as a pitcher. Not bad. I'm glad he's playing again. He sure loved baseball. Finks got him reading some book by Roger Angell and another called *Bang the Drum Slowly*, and then suggested that Hank get a fresh start at a game he obviously loved so much. Finks wouldn't know a baseball from a bowling ball, so I'm not sure why what he thought mattered, but it got Hank back in the game. That's good.

Hank walked over to the church with us, and Mom asked him to sit with us. He hesitated at first, but then said, "Yeah." I couldn't believe what I saw. Yellow St. Stephen's buses were parked by the church, and the entire brick walkway to the church was lined with blue blazers and khaki pants. The whole school—teachers, staff, and students—had come to St. George's. They couldn't all fit inside, so they just stood quietly outside. We went around to a side door and straight into the first pew. The place was packed, mostly it seemed, with those blue blazers. I got sort of choked up just seeing them all there. The organ was playing real loud and then stopped as we sat down. Stephie's casket was right near us in the aisle. It was smaller than your standard casket, and Mom started to weep looking at it. I held her hand and stared straight ahead. Hank had his head bowed.

And then from the back of the church came this voice:

"I am the resurrection and the life,
Saith the Lord: he that believeth
In me, though he were dead, yet shall
He live, and whosoever liveth and
Believeth in me, shall never die.

"Jesus called them unto him and said,
Suffer the little children to come
Unto me, and forbid them not: for
Of such is the kingdom of God.

"He should feed his flock like a shepherd: he shall
Gather the lambs with his arms, and carry them in his bosom."

He walked up the aisle saying this and we all stood. We remained standing for "The Lord is my Shepherd" and for "I will lift my eyes unto the hills," and then we sang "O God Our Help in Ages Past."

Jake

That was my only request for the service. The singing was so loud you could barely hear the organ, and it really got to me. I couldn't sing. I just stood there, listening.

The service blurred on me a little after that. I tried to pay attention, but I couldn't. Too many thoughts in my head, too many feelings all at once to focus very well. We prayed some, and there were lessons. Then, Ms. White spoke. She was brief, but good. I listened hard to her.

⁂

"We are here today to mourn together, to hold each other tight, to share our pain, and to comfort dear friends. Stephanie died too soon. We hurt deep down inside. Our friends, Karen and Jake, grieve for the bright-eyed wonderful child who was their daughter and sister. There is no satisfactory and sensible answer to why a child dies before her time. We cannot possibly know why a loving God would let this sort of tragedy happen. We are left with only two things: what we do know as true, and our faith.

"We know as true that Stephie was a blessing in the lives of all who knew her, especially her mother, brother, and stepbrother. She brightened the lives she touched. We are better for having known her and lucky to have shared her life. For this, we are grateful beyond words. This truth is ours to cherish forever. Our love for Stephie is eternal and undiminished. She lives in our hearts.

"Our faith tells us that Stephie lives again. She is God's child, and as God's child she will never die. We do not know what this means in a literal sense, but we do know that our faith gives us hope.

"Stephie's spirit is in us and with us and around us. Between our love, which we know as true, and our faith, which guides what we know, God is love. However difficult that is to feel in a time of terrible tragedy, one can feel the love in this church today. It enhances us all as a community in grief, but it also lifts us together as a community of love.

"God bless this community. God bless Jake and Karen. God bless Stephanie. And let us give thanks for the blessing of her life.

"Amen."

There were some more prayers, and we walked out of the church following Stephie, who was being carried by people from St. Stephen's. Joel was one of them. So was Mr. Meader. We walked down the brick path and through the cemetery to an open grave. When everybody had gathered around, we said another short prayer, and Mom, Hank, and I threw handfuls of dirt on the casket. Mom slipped down in her chair, and the minister said:

" . . . we commit the body of this child, Stephie, to the ground. The Lord bless her and keep her, the Lord make his face to shine upon her and be gracious unto her, the Lord lift up his countenance upon her, and give her peace, both now and evermore."

That was pretty much it. People had been told to go back to our house if they wanted. Hank and I took Mom by each arm, one of us on each side of her, and we walked her back to our car. I drove her home. Hank went off to find Mr. Finks.

There was food everywhere at home. A man outside was parking cars. There was a refreshment table with lemonade outside, and that's where the St. Stephen's students were hanging out. The grown-ups all went inside with the food. It was crowded in there. I found Hank inside and took him out to the lemonade table. Everyone was real awkward and quiet, so I kept introducing Hank to my friends. It gave us something to talk about. Hank's a pretty useful guy to have around sometimes.

Most of the rest of the day was a blur. Hank had to leave to catch a plane at about 4:00 p.m. We promised to do better at staying in touch. He was pretty emotional when he left, and that's a part of him that hasn't changed. I hope it never does. Everything is right up front with Hank. No bullshit. It used to get him in trouble.

⚬≈≈≈⚬

Shawn Gorman.

That's where most of my anger went in the weeks right after Stephie's death. The sound of the name made me sick with rage, the kind of rage that might make you crazy. Crazy enough to kill. Crazy enough to get a car and run him down and yell, "How's that feel, Shithead?!" I actually daydreamed about running him down like a dog, and then backing over him slowly, before running over him again. And again. And again.

He telephoned our house. I answered. "Hello," this real shaky voice said. "Can I speak to Mrs. Collins?"

"Who's calling?" I asked.

"Shawn Gorman," the voice almost sobbed out after a long pause.

"No!" I said. "No, you cannot speak to Mrs. Collins."

"OK," the voice said and hung up.

That was the day after Stephie's funeral. I heard later that he and his mother and father had been at the funeral service. It's a good thing I didn't know. I might have freaked out.

About a week after he called, I told Mom about it. Her reaction surprised me. "Poor boy," she said. "Poor, pathetic boy."

I told Mr. Meader about Shawn Gorman's call and his coming to the funeral. I told him how pissed I was. I told him I could kill the guy.

"I don't blame you, Jake," he said, leaning back in his chair the way he does. "That young man made the kind of stupid mistake, the kind of stupid decision, that can't be undone. There's no do-over; no three strikes. He screwed up big-time."

"No shit," I said.

Mr. Meader let out a big sigh and sat forward. He looked at me and said, "How do you suppose you'd be feeling about now, Jake, if you'd been out for a crazy after-school drive with some friends, and instead of having fun wound up killing somebody's child, somebody's little sister?"

"I'd feel like shit," I said, angry at his question. "But I didn't do anything like that. He did."

"That's true, Jake. That's true."

Looking back on that little talk with Mr. Meader, I know he made me think. Ms. White did, too. She called me into her office toward the end of April to "take my temperature," as she put it.

She got right down to business the way she almost always does. "How's your anger level, Jake? You still pretty hot under the collar?"

"Yup," I said.

"You've earned the right," she said. "But I want you to consider something, and I know it will be hard for you. Will you hear me out?"

"Yup," I said again.

"However justified anger may be, and in your case, it is entirely justified, it will wind up eating you away from the inside out. The only person hurt, ultimately, by your anger will be you, and the people who love you. Anger masks sadness. It prevents healing. It retards growth. There is nothing that it facilitates, not one positive thing. Anger is a relatively easy response to injustice, to wrong of any kind, and it easily transfers itself into bitterness and cynicism. It can take away your ability to appreciate good things, to offer love, to receive love. In other words, anger can impoverish you. That ends part one of my sermon."

"There's more?" I asked, irritated.

"A little bit. Part two is a question. Have you ever done something thoughtless, careless, stupid, or reckless? Shawn Gorman did. Stephie's dead. You are hurt. Your mother is devastated. All because he was behaving immaturely. He wasn't paying attention. He didn't think. Does any of that sound familiar?"

It did, but I said "no." I said, "He's a murderer and needs to suffer." I heard her, but I wasn't ready to accept what she was saying.

She asked about Mom, and we talked about baseball. Then I left the office. Over the last month, I thought lots about my conversations with Mr. Meader and Ms. White. I get now what it is they were saying. I'm just not sure I can shake off being angry. It was in yesterday's paper, though, that Shawn Gorman has been charged with manslaughter. He could spend a ton of time in jail. I didn't feel real happy about that news. I just felt nothing. He deserves whatever he gets, I thought, but I couldn't get into it like I thought I would. I could still hear Mom saying, "Poor boy. Poor, pathetic boy."

*

So I went back to school. There wasn't much else to do. Staying home would drive me crazy. I got back into the routine of lots of work, but nothing seemed normal, and Mom was real unpredictable. She'd seem fine one moment, and she'd lose it completely the next. Her late night visits to Stephie's room continue. I don't hear the sound as often, but off and on she'll make that pitiful noise. She's back at work, but she looks like a mess, the way she did last October. There are dark circles under her eyes, and she doesn't put on any make-up. She forgets things, too.

I've thought a lot about her. She pretty much has lived her life through us, and now one of us is dead. That leaves me—just me—to help her out. I'm not sure exactly how to do that. Ms. White and I have had long talks about it. She says I just need to show her I love her. Be there for her. Be consistent. And, Ms. White says, I need to take care of myself. If I'm OK, that will help Mom.

And I suppose I am doing OK. I'm not sure why that is. My sister's dead. My mother's fighting cancer, and even worse, she's now battling for . . . I don't know what exactly . . . perhaps it's her spirit or her mind or just her ability to cope. Except for Hank, we have no living relatives. I'm pretty alone in that sense.

I spend time with Mom on the weekends and in the evenings, but the rest of the time it's studying, baseball, and community service, over and over again, in a predictable routine. I see the same people every day—Meader, White, teachers, school friends. They all know what's happened. They don't say much about it. But I know they know.

What's next? Exams. Then summer. I'll play in the city baseball league. I got a job on the grounds crew here at school. That'll be good. Then back to school for eleventh grade, etc., etc., etc.

After St. Stephen's? It's hard to imagine. I have no clue really, but I'd bet that marine biology or some environmental thing will grab me. Given all the stuff going on in the world, maybe I'll join the service.

Jake

Maybe I'll go to the Naval Academy. Ha! Wouldn't Hank get a laugh out of that? But I read in the paper that a pro football player with a multi-million dollar contract quit to join up because it seemed like the right thing to do. He did it with his brother. He didn't make much noise about it. He just did it.

Whatever I do, it's got to have a point. Too many random, pointless events happen in my life, and I guess everybody's, that I can't control. I want to be in a group that knows what it cares about and does it well, has some focus, has some purpose. Stephie's death, Mom's cancer, the dead men in the water—there's no purpose there. It's nasty stuff. I know I can't escape it, but at least I can be part of something that has a goal, or a purpose, or a high sense of itself. Hell, all that's way too heavy to end this journal with. I need to lighten up. When I have to make those kinds of decisions, I'll go see Meader or White or someone, and they'll clue me in.

I didn't really know it until today, when I was watching that ceremony at Ground Zero, but I'm going to be fine. Stephie's dead. It's a fact, and it sucks. I'm alive. I didn't think that was so great at times over the last few weeks, but it beats the alternative.

It's two in the morning. I'm going to bed. Exams are coming. That stinks. I'm fielding fungoes from Mr. Meader tomorrow afternoon. Him, me, and three other guys. Joel is going to take me to a jazz club. He promised to do that last fall. I'm going to teach him how to fly fish. Ms. White says she wants to learn, too. She's going to come out to the Gunpowder with Mom and me on the first day after exams.

Acknowledgements

My most important thanks are due my wife, Phyllis, not only for her patience, love, and forbearance, but also for her superb administrative and artistic skills, without which *Jake* simply would not exist.

Deserved thanks also go to Washington College, particularly Chairman of the Board Jack Griswold; President John Toll; and Director of Admissions Kevin Coveney, for providing me with an office and marvelous setting in which to think and write. *Jake* happened on that beautiful little campus in Chestertown, Maryland, the only place to which George Washington explicitly gave his name.

Thank you to Asheville School in Asheville, North Carolina, which tolerates my writerly presumptions, and gives me the gift of serving the most generously kind institution I have had the experience of knowing. It is also nestled in one of the most beautiful settings imaginable.

For the example and inspiration provided to me, thanks to the International Boys' Schools Coalition and particularly to "the Conversation." My idealized Rector in *Jake* is some odd stew of Tony Jarvis, Rick Hawley, Dennis Campbell, Brad Gioia, Arnie Holtberg, John Bednall, Doug Blakey, Kerry Brennan, Rich Melvoin, Joe Cox, Charley Stillwell, Damon Bradley, Jake Dresden, and Vance Wilson. With leaders like these, our schools are in good hands.

Last but not least, thanks to Bruce Bortz and Elly Zupko for editing and publishing *Jake*. The opportunity is rare, but you have provided it.

Study Guide for Jake

These questions and topics may be used for classroom discussions, essays, or test questions.

WAYS THE SCHOOL IS RUN

- Rules, readings, assignments, motto, and projects
- Is it too much or not enough? Why?
- Advantages and disadvantages to these

THE SCHOOL AS A COMMUNITY

- This school functions as its own community. What do you think about that?
- Do you see other schools/organizations that work like this?
- Do you think more schools should be run like this?

CLASSES

- Taking all core classes versus core and electives
- How do you feel about not being able to choose classes in what you're interested in?

GRADING

- How do you decide what is an A, B, C, D, or F paper/assignment/student?

ATHLETICS

- Is it something everyone should participate in?
- What if someone doesn't want to be involved in anything?
- Should high schools admit some students based on athletics rather than scholastic aptitude?
- How do alumni play into this?

- Should students be allowed to miss classes because of athletics?
- What do you think of this school's idea of athletics?

REQUIRED COMMUNITY SERVICE

- Should you have to participate? Why/why not?

JOURNALS

- If you have nothing really to say, is it better to write about nothing or to copy Shakespeare or Socrates, etc.?

SEPTEMBER 11TH

- What did you feel about the "script" the students had to use when calling their parents? Is it too forced? Should you be allowed to ask and talk about what you want?

FACULTY AND STAFF

- Do they care more about their students in a smaller school?
- How comfortable would you be getting that personal attention from your teachers?

PUBLIC SCHOOL VERSUS PRIVATE SCHOOL

- Which is better? Why?
- Are they the same? Why?

EXPULSION

- What should be considered legitimate grounds for expulsion?
- Should Jake have been expelled? Should the other boys have been expelled?

PLAGIARISM

- Rules, punishment, definition, etc.

PREJUDICE

- Why do we judge people based on race, age, sex, etc.?
- Where do we learn this? Why do we pick up on this?
- Is it ok?

TUTORING AND STUDY SKILLS

- What are your feelings about these? Why?
- What do you think of someone/yourself if they/you go to tutoring?

ABORTION

- Pro-choice? Pro-life? Why?

BREAST CANCER

- Do women check themselves often enough?
- Prevention
- Treatments
- Genetics

SCHOOL PRIDE

- Is it important?
- Why do we care?
- What do you think about sportsmanship?
- Is there such a thing as too much pride?

STUDYING

- Importance
- Cheating and its effect

DEATH

- What about it saddens us the most?
- Considering everything he's been through, what do you think is allowing Jake to go on?
- How do you view life after you see death? What is its meaning?